Inferno

Book One

in the

Hell on Earth Series

by Violet E.C

Also by Violet E.C

A Collection of Romantic Short Stories

Dancing with Danger

Contents

Prologue
Chapter One: Escape
Chapter Two: Book of Aeternum
Chapter Three: Surprise Visit
Chapter Four: Sink or Swim
Chapter Five: Tension
Chapter Six: The Vicar
Chapter Seven: Secrets
Chapter Eight: The Depths of Hell
Chapter Nine: Fight or Flight
Chapter Ten: Hounds of Hell
Chapter Eleven: Earth, Heaven and Hell
Chapter Twelve: An Angel and A Demon Battle It Out In A Backyard
Chapter Thirteen: The Forbidden Fruit
Chapter Fourteen: Mourning
Chapter Fifteen: Ultimatum
Epilogue

First published on Great Britain in 2022
Copyright © Violet E.C 2022

1 2 3 4 5 6 7 8 9 10

Violet E.C has asserted her right under the Copyright, Designs and Patents Act, 1988, to be identified as Author of this work.
All rights reserved. No part of this publication may be reproduced or transmitted in any form or by any means, electronic or mechanical, including, photocopying, recording, or any information storage or retrieval system, without prior permission in writing from the Author.
This is a work of fiction. Names, characters, places and incidents either are products of the author's imagination or are used fictitiously. Any resemblance to actual events or locales or persons, living or dead, is entirely coincidental.

ASIN: B09RQXQ9GK
ISBN: 9798412177502
Imprint: Independently published

Playlist

ANGELS & DEMONS – jxdn
DEVILSH – Chase Atlantic
Hurts Like Hell – Madison Beer
Easier Than Lying – Halsey
Only Angel – Harry Styles
Drown – Bring Me The Horizon
Knife Under My Pillow – Maggie Lindemann
FLOOR 13 – Machine Gun Kelly
Ghost – Justin Bieber
Not Afraid Anymore – Halsey
Tension – Jack & Jack
Triggered – Chase Atlantic

Listen to this playlist on Spotify® using the Spotify Code below:

"Hell is empty and all the devils are here." —
William Shakespeare

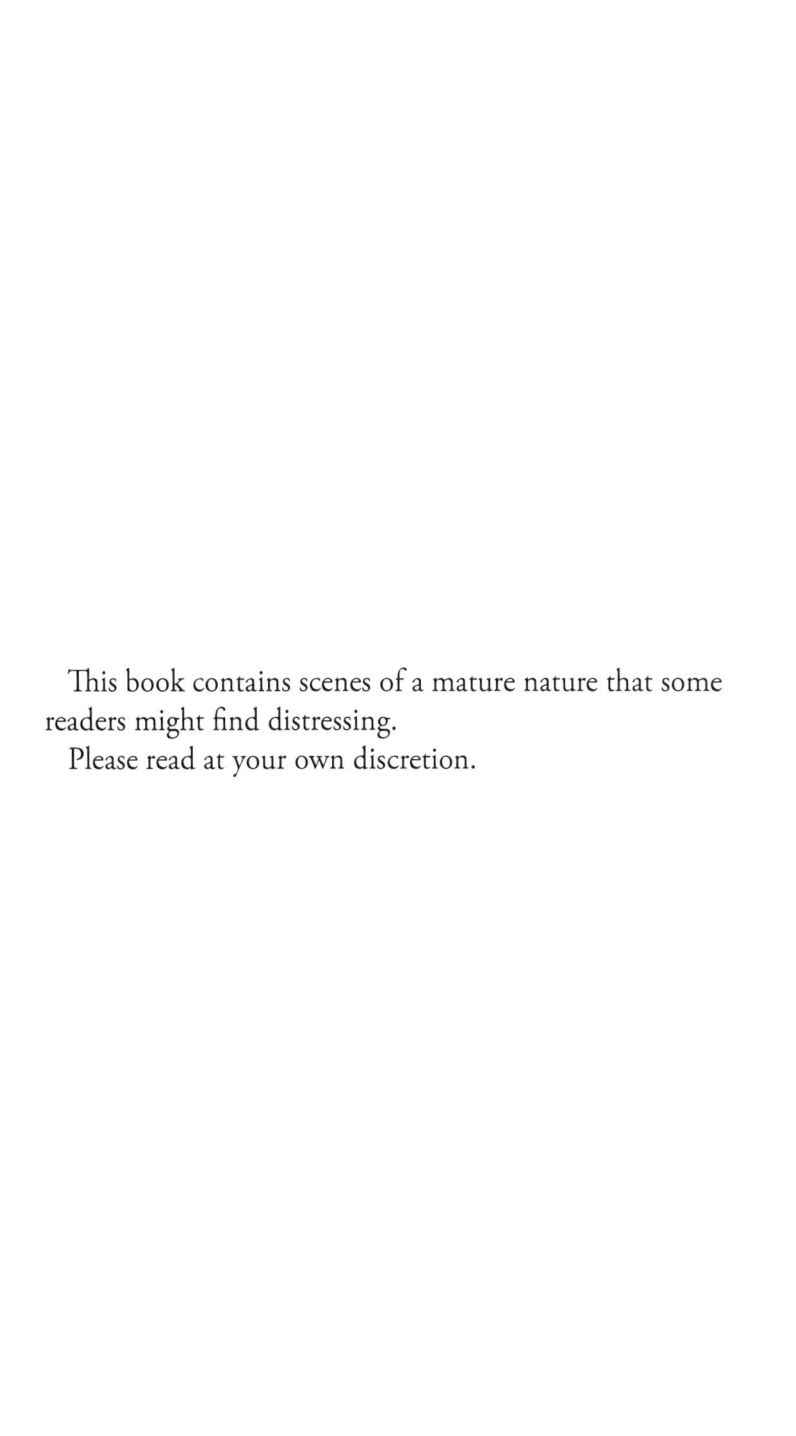

This book contains scenes of a mature nature that some readers might find distressing.

Please read at your own discretion.

Inferno

Prologue

The dark-haired woman paced around a large room, scowling. A glass cube, the size of a small box lay upon her desk; its bright colors swirled around the room, creating a kaleidoscopic effect that bounced off the dark stone walls and reflected off the large glass jars that were lined up on the shelves and filled with suspicious-looking items, suspended in murky liquid.

"It can't be true." She murmured angrily to herself, turning to face the cube. Her robes, which were a deep purple and black, swished behind her elegantly, brushing the stone floors.

"Tell me it isn't true!" Her voice rose, objects in the room rattled in their places as she slammed her hands down onto the desk in anger. The furniture shuddered and cracked, her hands leaving perfect fist-shaped dents in the dark wood.

"The future is unclear, but the prophecy remains certain." A voice emanated from the cube, it was raspy and strained, like someone who'd spoken too much when they had a sore throat.

"Then I'll make sure it never comes to fruition." She snarled and turned away from the box.

She perched on the edge of the desk, mulling the idea over in her mind. Her long black nails, which were more like talons upon closer inspection, tapped on the desk in an erratic rhythm while her face was a mask of thought.

A sudden knock on the door interrupted her reverie.

"Enter." She snapped.

A small, fat creature emerged, dressed in a dark robe. It had gnarled horns protruding from its head, similar to a ram's and its skin was blue and scaly, like a lizard. It kept its eyes trained on the ground and hovered in the doorway, as if it were afraid to take even a step into the room.

"Yes?" The woman prompted, her eyebrow arched, obvious frustration at the intrusion written on her face.

"He's asking for you."

"Well you're the nurse, aren't you? You look after him. Isn't that what you're here for?" She rolled her eyes, ready to dismiss the irritating creature.

"Not your son." It swallowed thickly, eyes pinned to the stone floor. "The King, my lady, the King is asking for you." The creature fumbled with its robe, twisting the material around its stubby fingers and then letting it fall down repeatedly.

The woman's head snapped up, eyes narrowing as she stepped around the desk to the creature in the doorway.

"Did he say why?"

It shook its head, eyes still cast down.

"No, my lady. He didn't."

The dark haired woman took a deep breath and composed herself, smoothing out any wrinkles in her robe. She picked up the cube and placed it in a wooden box, the light dimming as she locked it and tucked it away under her desk.

With the flick of her hand and dark smoke tendrils trickling out from her fingers, the dents in the desk smoothed out, leaving no trace of her outburst.

With her chin up, head held high, she strode to the door, glaring down at the creature expectantly.

"Well, it better be important."

And it was. The King was, in fact, dead.

Chapter One: Escape

Ten Years Ago

The hallways buzzed with a flurry of students, as the bell rang and the classes were dismissed for the day. Students flooded the corridor in a hurry to leave the dingy building that was Neverfield High School.

Mary sat on the closed toilet lid, staring at the graffitied door of the stall, clutching her bag strap as she listened to the hubbub outside. She hated the crowds, the noisy students, and the slamming of the hollow, metal locker doors, but most of all, she *hated* Dante Enfer; her own personal bully who created her own personal Hell whenever he could... Which meant basically every waking moment at school.

Dante was an all-around bad boy; with his leather jackets, inky black hair, insanely sculpted torso, and his motorcycle, he made all the girls swoon and all the guys green with envy. He had everyone's attention, was good at pretty much anything he tried, plus he had looks to die for. Literally.

Inferno

For some reason unknown to Mary, Dante loved to pick on her and only her. At first, she thought it was because she was quiet, worked hard, and didn't cause any trouble. Then she considered that maybe he was dumb and he was picking on her because she was smart. But when she saw his test scores in class, that debunked her theory. She couldn't understand why he had such a vendetta against her, but she'd stopped trying to understand a while ago. Dante was a mystery she wasn't willing to solve.

She mainly tried to avoid him like the plague. In the beginning, her grades had suffered because she flunked every class she shared with him, which she quickly realized was nearly all of them. How was it that they had almost the exact same schedule?!

So she settled for just laying low, getting to class on time so Dante couldn't tease her before the teacher arrived, and leaving exactly when the bell rang, so she could be out and into the next class before he could lay a finger on her. And if she had spare time? The girls' bathroom seemed like a safe place to go.

However, today, she needed to get home to her dad so she could help him cook dinner for the pastor and his wife from the neighboring town. Every month, her dad hosted a dinner, mainly for the local pastors, but sometimes for the Mayor or the Sheriff. Her dad was a social butterfly in the community, unlike Mary who tended to prefer her own company.

She couldn't be late this time, so she took a deep breath and darted out of the bathroom, into the throng of smelly, overexcited teenagers. Normally she'd have Ally, her trusted sidekick and best friend who was, if not a bit weird and experimental, her most loyal and truest friend.

Her extracurricular activities aside, she was a badass chick who'd kick some serious butt if Mary asked her to. All butt

Violet E.C

apart from Dante's however, because though she didn't like him, she believed it was better to be at the right hand of the Devil instead of his enemy, so she was civil with him. Plus she said he was "too hot" to be mean, whatever that meant.

But today Ally was with her boyfriend Mark, skipping classes. *They're probably somewhere getting high and having sex in the back of his crappy car.* Mary grumbled as she pushed in front of a tall boy who was blocking her path.

Mark was what Mary considered a bad influence, he was friends with Dante and his boy band gang so she didn't approve, but Ally was head over heels, so all Mary could do was smile and feign interest when her best friend rattled on about all the "cool" things Mark did.

It was February, so partway through the semester. The weather was cool, but not freezing cold, even so, Mary pulled her jacket tighter as she navigated the halls.

She'd heard along the grapevine that a party was happening at Jesse's-another of Dante's minions- on Saturday. She couldn't care less for him but she did like parties, so maybe she'd show face for a couple of hours for free food and good music.

Whilst contemplating the party and what she'd wear, Mary made a beeline for her locker, hastily pushing her way through the crowd. Boys were whooping, laughing and high-fiving. Girls were giggling and discussing their weekend plans. It was the usual high school scene.

Her locker was in sight and she breathed a sigh of relief at the blue metal door. She could be out of the school building in the next few minutes and on her way home for the weekend. Just as she squeezed past some skaters lounging around the lockers, a leather jacket, and t-shirt-clad, broad chest blocked her path. Mary internally groaned, steeling herself for more teasing and bullying from the Devil.

Inferno

So close and yet so far away from freedom for the weekend, Mary swallowed thickly as she stared at the floor, refusing to make eye contact.

"Where you off to Mary Mary, quite contrary?" Dante always mocked her name, saying it with a distaste that made her clench her teeth in anger. She stayed silent, mentally thinking up ways to murder Dante; ballpoint pen to the eye, heavy chemistry book to the head...

"Got nothing to say?" He interrupted her murderous thoughts. "But Mary Mack, you always have an answer for everything."

Mary stared into his chest, she would *not* meet his cruel eyes.

All he ever did was mock her.

She never stood up to him though, telling herself not to stoop to his level and that he'd get bored of her if she gave him no reaction. It'd worked in the past, but recently, it was difficult to pretend like he wasn't bothering her. It was *every freaking day.*

Dante ran his eyes over Mary's small form, taking in her halo of white-blonde hair scrunched up into a messy bun on top of her head, her jacket and jeans, her white knuckles as she tightly gripped the books in her hands.

Her downcast eyes stared at the floor and he resisted the urge to pull her chin up to meet his. He wanted her attention, he wanted her eyes on him, he wanted to see sweet hurt in her honey gaze when he called her mean names. Yep, he was a dickhead.

Dante balled his fist, his nails digging into his palms. He'd resist touching her. *For now.*

"If you want to get to your locker, then you need to know the password." Jesse, Dante's right-hand man, had the personality of a middle schooler. His jokes were immature and

Violet E.C

dumb, but they made Mary feel like an idiot nonetheless.

She sighed and turned on her heel, deciding that she could forfeit her other books and catch up on homework early on Monday morning.

However, Dante was not letting her go without a fight, and he quickly stepped in front of her, blocking her other exit.

Dante's eyes were alight with cruel excitement, he loved to rile Mary up and by the sound of her quickened heartbeat, he knew she was starting to panic. A wicked smile stretched across his cheeks.

Mary ground down her teeth and turned around, she quickly darted for the locker again, her shoes squeaking on the Lino floor. Dante was faster. *Always faster.*

Exasperated, Mary pushed against his arm which stuck out as he leaned against the wall. His arm was like solid metal, it had no give and Mary wanted to sink her nails into the sleeve of his leather jacket and tear it off. She wanted to make him bleed for all his mean jabs and bullying behavior. She wanted to scream in frustration as these idiot boys made her feel like shit. A crowd was forming around the two of them, high schoolers looking for any drama in their lives and hoping for a fight.

After burning a mental hole into Dante's t-shirt, Mary tilted her chin up and finally met his eyes for a brief second. Her heart beat a little too quickly as his dark, smug gaze burned into hers and she blamed it on the situation, rather than acknowledging his good looks.

Thick, dark curls brushed the collar of his jacket, framing his face. His angular jawline, perfectly straight nose and heavy brows accentuated his piercing eyes. He really was a work of art.

He's a bully and I'm his victim, she reminded herself. *It doesn't matter how hot he is. He's still a jackass.* Her gaze fell back to

Inferno

his chest as anger simmered in her blood.

A lazy smile covered Dante's full lips, his eyes glinting with enjoyment as he challenged her. A quick look at her silver eyes showed him a slight look of defiance mixed with fear. Exactly what he was looking for.

They stood in stalemate and Dante grinned at his friends, knowing they enjoyed teasing Mary as much as he did. They laughed back and the group of high school kids around them watched on.

"Just leave me alone," Mary mumbled quietly, tired of fighting. She just wanted to go home, curl up in her bed and never leave the house again.

"I didn't catch that. What did you say?" Dante's voice was obnoxious and loud, a few students snickered.

"Leave me alone," Mary said, her voice a bit louder this time. She didn't dare punctuate her words too much in case he decided taunting wasn't enough and started physical violence. She didn't know how far he would take his bullying and she wasn't planning on finding out any time soon.

Stooping down to her level, Dante got up close to Mary's face. She held her breath, heart thumping in her chest, terrified of what he might do. She could smell cigarettes on his breath, the musky aftershave he wore, the distinct scent of leather from his jacket. His hand snaked forward and he gripped her chin hard, hard enough to bruise. His skin felt hot and electric on her own and Mary tried not to think about how much his touch affected her.

It's fear, that's all. Nothing more, nothing less. She chanted over and over in her head in an attempt to calm her wild heart.

She was forced to look at his eyes again, and her heart thundered at his smoldering charcoal with a ring of red around the iris- a color she'd never seen in anyone else. Dante's eyes were unique, only his, just like her own silver ones. Her gaze accidentally dropped to his full lips and she quickly looked away, jerking her chin from his vice-like grip, pretending like he wasn't bruising her milky skin.

Dante's eyes blazed, he was enjoying his little game. Riling Mary up was his favorite pastime. Yeah, he could get any girl in school, but it seemed that Mary was immune to his good looks and bad-boy charm, and that meant a challenge. Which he had yet to conquer.

"Make me." He whispered in her ear, his hot breath tickling her skin.

Mary blushed furiously, angry at herself for talking back at him, challenging him in his stupid games. She'd escalated it and that was stupid. This was the first time she'd actually stood up to him and unluckily for her, he loved it.

"Whatcha gonna do, Mary Mack?"

She clenched her jaw at his nickname, silently cursing the world for putting Dante on this Earth at the exact same time as her. Her fists trembled and she gripped her books so tightly that the hard edges dug into her palms painfully. She felt her skin get hot under her clothes like she was burning up. Glancing down at herself, she noticed a faint glow on her skin. No one else would've noticed, but she did.

This had been happening more often than not, but she'd been keeping it quiet, perhaps it was the fluorescents? *Best to blame it on the lights than end up in the nuthouse for saying you have glowing skin,* she willed herself to calm down. She needed to get out of there and fast. She didn't need anyone else noticing the weird glowing thing right now.

In a flash decision, with no hesitation, she shoved Dante's chest.

Hard.

Her push caught him by surprise and caused him to stumble backward into the lockers with a metallic thud. Without checking to see if she'd managed to cause any damage, Mary legged it in the opposite direction as fast as she could.

The crowd of students parted for her like the Red Sea and she sprinted out of the double doors that led to the car park, shoes skidding on the concrete. Her heart thudded, her breath coming out in short puffs as adrenaline spurred her on. Without looking back in fear of seeing Dante's face again, she spotted the yellow bus and leaped onto it, taking the steps two at a time, not stopping until she was all the way at the back.

Her chest heaved with adrenaline and fear. God, why had she done that? Why did she have to shove Dante? She mentally cursed herself for being so stupid.

She slid down in her cracked, vinyl seat, trying to remain inconspicuous and she opened a book in her hands, pretending to read, but also covering her face in case Dante decided to check the bus.

Her heart jackhammered in her chest as she watched the bus door around the edges of her biology book, anticipating Dante to appear at any moment and drag her off as she clawed at the sticky vinyl seats, leaving nail marks down the bus's interior. Exactly like a horror movie.

Luckily, the bus lurched forward and turned around, driving away from the school before her imagination could create any more cliché high school horror scenes.

Mary hesitantly glanced over her shoulder, back at the school entrance and her eyes caught Dante's. He was standing at the double doors, arms folded across his broad chest, eyes narrowed to slits, his mouth set in a hard line.

Do you know that saying "don't poke a bear"?

Well, Mary had just hit a very angry bear with a taste for payback and she was first on his hit list.

Chapter Two: Book of Aeternum

Ten Years Ago

The kitchen smelt delicious as Mary wandered in. She'd got home late, despite escaping Dante and his hoard. She apologized a hundred times to her dad before going to shower, and emerging in her more formal clothes for dinner with guests.

Her dad, Alan, a middle-aged man with grey streaks in his light brown hair, pushed his glasses up his nose as he stirred a pot of bubbling liquid.

"So what's on the menu tonight?" Mary asked, as she grabbed an apron and tied it around her back, keeping her nicer clothes clean as she got ready to help her dad.

"The usual." He replied as he leafed through a recipe book on the nearby counter. He'd learned to adapt after Mary's mom had passed away when she was little and they fell into a routine together.

He didn't speak much of his late wife, except for when Mary asked, which had been often when she was a kid. She'd learned every story about her mom off by heart; how her parents met, what their first date was, and when they'd got married.

But as she grew up, Mary saw how much it hurt her father to keep bringing his late wife up, so she slowly stopped asking, pretending that she was okay only knowing half of the story. Her heart ached when she saw the breathtaking woman in pictures; a beautiful stranger.

Mary looked exactly like her mom; white hair, white skin, and silver eyes with golden flecks in the iris. She'd often been questioned about them at school, to which she answered that they were costume contact lenses.

When she was little, kids used to tease her about her eyes and her hair. She didn't like being different. So when she got to high school, Mary learned that lying about them and saying they were contacts or that her silver hair was a fun hair dye, was much easier than telling the truth and being an outcast.

Mary often wondered if it pained her dad to look at his daughter and see an exact replica of his dead wife. Every day Mary grew more and more to look like her mom. Maybe that was why her dad spent so much time in the church or burying himself in hundreds of books in his office, maybe he found it hard to be around her.

Perhaps that was part of the reason why Mary was so keen to leave Neverfield. She felt trapped here, her dad not wanting to spend an excessive amount of time with her, preferring his books to her company. He still loved her of course, but the town felt suffocating for her.

She needed freedom. Which was exactly what she was going to do once she graduated at the end of the year. She'd be free of this town and off to the city where she could start a new life and no longer be sad Mary with silver eyes and a dead mom.

The doorbell rang, breaking her thoughts and her dad glanced up at the clock as he stirred.

"Hmm, they're early. Can you get them drinks while I finish up here? Just offer drinks and make some small talk." Her dad turned to the fridge to find an ingredient and Mary dutifully hung up her apron and plodded to the front door.

A small, pink-cheeked man and a podgy woman were on the other side, they introduced themselves as Pastor Nolan and his wife Jean.

They took a seat in the living room, accepting drinks and Mary left them commenting on how nice the furniture was.

She brought back drinks and sat quietly, pretending to be interested in the conversation about the upholstery of the couch.

Her dad rescued her before she died from boredom and they sat to eat at the large dining table in their kitchen. The small talk dragged on, Pastor Nolan was obviously kissing ass about their house. It was no secret that Mary and her dad lived comfortably, Mary'd never questioned why, but now she wondered if other pastors didn't live so nicely.

The conversation lulled and she stared at her plate, pushing around the potatoes with her fork and watching them roll back and forth on the fine china her dad brought out for guests.

Dante's antics today had put her in a mood, she was worried he'd turn up at her house in the middle of the night to get his own back and that thought alone made her stomach churn, her appetite non-existent.

"Pastor Nolan, I wonder if you have the Book of Aeternum in your church?" Her father asked, breaking the silence. The pastor's head popped up from looking at his plate, a look of confusion painted on his round face.

Inferno

"I'd love to give you good news, Pastor Lux but that book hasn't been seen for seventeen years. It went missing- presumed stolen, before my time at the church. It was never returned."

Mary turned to her dad, suddenly interested in the conversation. Why was her dad so keen to get his hands on this book? He'd asked the last two pastors who came for dinner the exact same question. It seemed that there had only been one copy of this Book of Aeternum and it had been entrusted to the town of Ecclesia, which was the founding town in their state. It had the oldest and biggest church and therefore housed all the important artifacts.

"That's a shame to hear that. I remember hearing of it being stolen and I hoped it had found its way back home."

Pastor Nolan shook his head solemnly whilst chewing on a large mouthful, he swallowed and Mary keenly watched him, eager to hear his response.

"Unfortunately not. We scour the Internet and call book stores in the state every day but so far, it hasn't turned up. We've started to wonder whether it even exists anymore."

"But there are no other copies?" Her father asked, watching the pastor intently. His face gave nothing away and Mary's eyes flew back and forth between the two.

"They didn't make any. The Book of Aeternum was one of a kind. It is believed that it wasn't written here on Earth. Now whether you believe that, that's another conversation." He laughed jollily, not taking his words seriously and his wife joined in.

Her father nodded in agreement, smiling tightly and they moved onto lighter topics.

Mary was lost in thought. What did Pastor Nolan mean by "wasn't written here on Earth"? Was he implying that some believe another being wrote it in some other realm? Was that

even possible?
　What was going on?

Chapter Three: Surprise Visit

Present Day

Mary's heels clicked on the floor as she strolled confidently through the office, heading straight for the elevator. She'd sealed yet another sale and was thrilled. The couple had been indecisive about the house on 4th and West, but with a little convincing on the prime location and great yard space, they'd finally gone through with it.

She'd got the paperwork sorted and sent out straight away. So now, she decided to take the rest of the day off as a treat for working so hard. Maybe she'd hit up a friend in the city and they'd go to the spa. *Yeah, a spa day sounded just perfect.*

"Mary?"

Her daydream about massages and face masks fizzled out as Mary turned back to see her boss; Monica beckoning her from the doorway of her office.

"A quick word before you go."

"Of course." Mary followed Monica- a power-hungry real estate broker who founded the business- into her skyrise office. A wall of glass overlooked the sprawling city below, a large leather couch sat at one wall while a bookshelf that rivaled a library was on the other. It was an impressive space and something Mary aspired for herself.

Monica settled behind her large desk, gesturing for Mary to take a seat.

"Firstly, Mary, can I say how impressed I've been recently? Your numbers are looking great, you're getting new clients who fit our image and I'm glad that you've made such progress here."

A genuine smile broke out on Mary's face. She'd been working her ass off for this job, lots of late nights and coffee had helped her secure deals which could have fallen through in the wrong hands. Finally, it had paid off.

"Thank you, Monica, that means a lot."

Monica nodded, smiling kindly, and opened her mouth to speak again when a knock on the door interrupted her.

"Come in." She called.

The door opened and Mary turned to see Monica's secretary, poking her head around the door.

"Your 2 o'clock is here."

Monica nodded and Mary turned back to face her.

"And because you've been doing so well Mary, I'd like you to show our new employee the ropes."

Her eyes widened, *show someone the ropes?* That was a big task and not something Monica would've dealt out lightly. It was a huge deal.

"Of course, I'd be honored to." Mary grinned, unable to contain her excitement at getting such an important job placed in front of her.

Next up, promotion time. She smiled internally at the prospect of a pay rise and possibly a bigger office.

Life had been going swimmingly in her job recently. Her love life and family relations left something to be desired, but

Inferno

she threw herself into her work and it paid off. She had a fat salary, happy clients, and slept well at night knowing she was on the up.

The familiar scent of cigarettes and leather floated into the room and Mary's stomach churned, her breakfast threatening to come back up to say hello.

No.

Panic made the blood in her veins ice cold and her heart pounded in her chest.

It can't be.

With every quickened heartbeat, she felt adrenaline pump in her blood, making her jittery and nervous.

No way.

Her skin prickled, her mouth dry and she thought she might faint or worse, vomit.

Not after what happened, he can't be back.

Taking a deep breath, she quickly glanced at the door and instantly wished she hadn't.

He stood there, tall and menacing, still wearing his signature leather jacket. But he'd swapped out his t-shirts for a crisp black shirt and his biker boots for formal black shoes. His dark hair was cut shorter and pushed off his face, showing his amazing bone structure. He sported new glasses, dark frames that accentuated his high cheekbones. And those eyes. Those dark eyes that burned a hole in Mary's soul.

Dante Enfer.

Mary blinked a few times, making sure she wasn't in some nightmare. Nope, Dante still stood in the doorway, blocking her escape as usual and suddenly she was thrown back to her high school memories where he'd constantly stand in her way and tease her.

"Mary, I'd like to introduce you to Dante, he's new at the firm and wants to get to know the business. So I thought who better than our highest ranking team member this month?" Monica smiled, obviously elated with her choice of pairing while Mary's stomach rolled like she'd swallowed acid. She tentatively took a step towards the door so she didn't look like a bitch, even though every cell in her body was telling her to run for the hills.

Dante's black eyes burned into Mary's, her skin felt ablaze and her instincts told her to get out as fast as she could. *If only.*

"Dante, Mary is one of our most valued brokers and will be showing you the ropes in this business."

He stepped forward, reaching out his hand and extending it to Mary. A friendly enough gesture that didn't match the sinister glint in his eyes.

"Great to see you, Ms. Lux."

Dante looked down at her, assessing this new Mary. She was different to the one he'd grown used to, the one he constantly thought about, fantasized about. But he wasn't complaining, this was a new and improved Mary and he was ready to get to know every part of her.

Mary stiffly stuck out her hand to meet his, smiling mechanically but not meeting his eyes. She knew all too well what they looked like and what dark thoughts they showed.

"And you too."

His hot skin enveloped her cool hand, making her whole body set alight. It had been years since they touched and every inch of her skin felt hyper-aware. Her pulse raced, her blood bubbling and making her feel hot. She gritted her teeth as his scent invaded her senses again, making her clench her thighs and feeling a flush blossom under her skin.

What is wrong with me? She questioned herself, mad at her body's betrayal. *Less than five minutes into a less-than-ideal situation with my childhood bully and I'm turned on? Get a grip,* she chided herself.

His eyes roamed her as he held her hand. Dante noted her hair color, her posture, her figure. It'd been ten years, of course, she'd grown up and the way she looked right now in that tight skirt, sheer blouse, and red-bottomed heels made him have to resist the urge to adjust his pants in front of everyone.

Monica grinned pleased with her own decision, she gestured for them to sit down at the desk, so oblivious to the tension between Mary and Dante.

Dante pulled his hand away first, smirking, and flopped down in one of the chairs. It was simple for him to pretend that he was an easy-going, cool guy. Monica had no idea of his past and he was betting that Mary was still too shy to speak up.

She sat on the edge of her seat, nervous energy making her twitchy as she forced herself to sit still, although everything in her body was still screaming at her to make a run for the door while they were distracted.

"So, Mary I'll get an extra desk for your office for Dante to shadow you. If you can take him to a couple of your viewings and show him, around that would be great. It'll only take him a few weeks to settle but with your help, I'm sure he'll fit right into the firm." She smiled kindly and Mary nodded, unable to form any coherent words.

God, why, why, why? She mentally cursed the skies for making this alignment happen, she thought she'd escaped Hell when she left Neverfield, but it came looking for her.

While Dante and Monica talked logistics, Mary planned her escape from him. For now, she'd have to show him around, but she didn't have to be nice to him. The bare minimum and he would be out of her hair in a few weeks, even less may be.

Or so she hoped.

Violet E.C

She knew he was a fast learner from school, hopefully, that would be to her advantage. Although nothing with Dante was easy and she knew he had an ulterior motive, the look on his face didn't say this was a chance meeting.

"Really? That's amazing." Mary zoned back in to hear Monica's surprised tone.

"Mary, you didn't mention that you and Dante went to high school together." Panicking about what she'd missed in the conversation, Mary avoided Dante's burning gaze from her left and kept her eyes on Monica.

"We barely knew each other."

"We hung out a lot." Dante corrected her and she had the strongest urge to glare at him. He smirked, watching Mary visibly tense up at the sound of his voice.

This is gonna be fun, he thought to himself. He grinned at Monica, charming his way into her office had been too easy and now he'd be working with Mary every day? Could his plan get any better?

"Oh, well that's great, you two can have a catch-up lunch then, Mary was just headed out, weren't you?"

She considered Monica a good boss, but at that moment, Mary could have leaped across that ridiculously expensive desk and strangled her blue at the suggestion of lunch with Dante Enfer; the Devil incarnate.

"That would be great, I'm new to the city, maybe she could show me around too?"

Mary spun in her seat, looking incredulously to Dante whose face sported a shit-eating grin.

He knows exactly what he's doing, that asshole. Mary tried so hard to maintain her composure, but the walls she'd built were crumbling.

Monica nodded enthusiastically at Dante's request and Mary considered throwing herself out of that beautiful skyline

Inferno

view window and splattering herself on the hard concrete below. At least it would save her from this torture.

"Sure." Mary gritted out, teeth clenched so hard her skull ached.

Dante rose out of his chair, shaking Monica's hand firmly with the most charming grin, and turned to Mary.

"Lead the way, Mary Mack."

Chapter Four: Sink Or Swim

Ten Years Ago

The bass thudded in Mary's ears as she walked up the street to the party. Jesse lived a few blocks away, so she'd decided walking was probably easier than asking a classmate for a ride, then if she wanted to make a quick escape she could run home, especially if she happened to run into the Devil himself.

She pushed open the already ajar front door, to reveal the get-together already in full swing. The living room was stuffed full of sweaty teenagers dancing to the pulsing beat. Squeezing past the bodies to get through to the kitchen, she found a group from her class in there. She grabbed a plastic red cup off the counter and sloshed some strong liquor in it before filling it to the brim with a mixer.

After greeting a few people and making idle chat- she wasn't exactly best friends with any of those people, she poured herself another drink or two and went to find Ally. Mary was sure she'd be there in the thick of the party, crushed between

Inferno

damp, grabby bodies and loving every second of it.

With dimmed lights, it was hard to make out faces in the dark room, the music pulsed and the alcohol in her system made her vision less than 20/20. Mary stumbled through the crowd, she'd only had one drink, right? Or was it two, maybe three? Who was counting anyway? She was there to party and it wasn't like she was driving anywhere.

Mary giggled, putting her hand in front of her face and laughing at her fingers which seemed to swirl around. She laughed harder as she looked around, suddenly finding everything very funny.

Cup in hand, Mary stood on her tiptoes, trying to spot Ally between the mass of bodies. She had no luck though, the crowd was thick and she couldn't discern faces from arms and legs in the darkness.

Rolling back on her heels too quickly, Mary stumbled, tripping over and falling right into the person behind her. She turned to apologize, sloshing her drink everywhere including on multiple feet. She bit her lip to stop herself from giggling at the alcohol-stained pairs of shoes in front of her.

Looking up, suddenly her eyes met dark ones, circled with a ring of red.

Her giggles died in her throat as she swallowed hard. *Oh man, of all the drunk teenagers to bump into, into, it had to be him.* Sometimes Mary wondered if the universe and the powers that be really hated her.

His eyes went from pissed off to amused when he saw who had bumped into him, a sinister grin stretched across his dark features. Mary gulped audibly, suddenly feeling a lot less giddy than before.

"Would you look at that? Mother Mary's at a party, not praying at home with daddy, how sweet." His mocking tone made Mary's teeth grind together. His minions laughed around him, eyes on her like a pack of hyenas looking at their prey. Grinning wickedly and almost salivating.

She hadn't forgotten yesterday's incident; pushing Dante over. And she was betting he hadn't either if the look in his eyes was anything to go by. She knew she'd be paying for it tonight.

"What do you want, Dante?" Mary challenged him. The copious amounts of alcohol that she consumed tonight were making her bolder than usual.

"Well, after your little tantrum yesterday, I think an apology is due."

Mary sighed and looked up at Dante, suddenly not scared to meet his eye. He was dressed in all black- as usual, his unruly, dark hair brushed over his forehead. He really was the epitome of a bad-boy; he oozed darkness and danger. Most of the girls at school found it attractive, but every cell in Mary's body screamed at her to run away. Or at least, *nearly* every cell.

Her heart beat a little faster as her mind wandered to what Dante would look like with his hair pushed off his face. What he'd look like with *her* pushing his hair off his face. Her eyes traveled to his lips, she faintly considered what they'd feel like. He'd be a rough kisser, that's for sure. He wouldn't hold back as he pressed his lips to hers, practically forcing his tongue in her mouth as he held her head with his large hands, impatient fingers weaved into her soft hair. And she'd let him kiss her of course, her mouth would fall open for his kiss, practically begging for it…

God, why was she thinking like that? Alcohol made her brain think the worst things at the worst times.

Dante stared at her, Mary's wandering gaze made him almost forget his words. Her silver eyes burned into his lips, hers parted gently, a breath rushing out from them and he saw

Inferno

a faint blush crawl up her neck in the dark room. It wasn't hard to guess what she was thinking and man, did he feel it too. A mixture of attraction and something else, something darker.

Mary snapped out of her alcohol-induced daydream and quickly diverted her gaze to the floor. She was embarrassed to be caught ogling Dante when she tried so hard to be immune to his good looks. He watched her expectantly, one dark eyebrow arched under his hair. He'd moved closer, his shoulders inches from her face, making her crane her neck to see his face.

"Fine, I'm sorry." She gritted out, her words dripping with acid and not sounding sorry at all. For some reason- probably the many drinks she'd had- Mary decided tonight was the night to roll the dice. *Let's see what Dante would really do if I antagonized him, just a little,* she smirked.

Dante shook his head, dark humor in his eyes as he gazed at her almost ethereal form. She wore white and Dante smiled at the irony. He, in all black and she, a vision in white. Light and dark. Complete opposites.

Mary's skin glowed faintly in the dim lights, her hair like a halo framing her face and those eyes. He wanted to touch her, wanted to get closer. Those pools of liquid starlight pierced his own. He felt like he was on fire when she met his eyes, and the things he wanted to do to her, in the dark of the room, what he wanted her to feel... The edge between pain and pleasure, he knew she wasn't the good girl that had everyone fooled, he knew she'd be begging for it.

"No, no, Mary Mack, say it like you mean it."

Mary resisted the temptation to roll her eyes. God, this man child was really begging for her to punch him a new one. She stared at the wall behind his ear, avoiding his smoldering black eyes. Her mind was fuzzy, he was crowding her space,

invading her every thought, his scent clouding her mind.
"Okay then, I'm sorry."
"For?"
He cocked an eyebrow and she clenched her fist, so incredibly tempted to smack that particular feature right off his damn pretty face. She could feel his breath on her face, her skin tingled at the heat.
"Pushing you in the hall."
"And?"
An unnerving smirk was etched into his full lips, Mary stared at them rather than meeting his eyes. Dante wanted her to look up and meet his own, he craved the burn, her intense gaze, the way her eyes made him feel. But she didn't. He stepped closer, so that her chest brushed against his, the blood in his veins buzzed in anticipation.
"And what?" She challenged.
One thing Dante Enfer didn't like was being denied. *Anything*. He liked people to bend to his will, he played the games on his own terms and he didn't like Mary's nerve.
"And for standing up for yourself. Don't try to be anything more than you are Mother Mary. You're just a God-loving daddy's girl and it's pathetic." He spat, his words cut like a knife.
All the humor was gone from his eyes. The game had taken a rough turn and Mary didn't want to play anymore.
She stepped back, not expecting his words to hurt so much. Not that she sought out Dante's approval, she didn't really care what he thought, but she also didn't know why he despised her so much. Religion was a community in this town, not just her and her dad. He never picked on anyone else who went to church. Then again, he rarely picked on anyone else as often as he did her.
"Now we all know why Mommy couldn't stand to stay here

Inferno

with you. Because you're a pathetic little girl, Mary Mack."

At the mention of her mother, anger set alight in her veins. It coursed through her body, lighting her skin and making her almost luminescent. How dare he talk about her mom like that!

Mary's rage filled her body like a wildfire, burning every cell of her body in a wave of white hot anger that sought out punishment. Dante would pay for what he said, he had no right bringing her mother up. It was a sensitive topic on the best of days, and he didn't want to know what Mary was like on the worst.

He watched her as she seemed to illuminate, her body emitting a gentle glow under the surface of her skin. He'd think it was impossible but then again, he'd seen crazier stuff than a glowing girl. He was intrigued and he smiled smugly as he knew he'd hit a nerve. Getting Mary riled up was his favorite pastime after all.

Without a second thought, Mary's hand flew across his cheek. The slap rang out and died down quickly, swallowed up by the loud music. Dante's face snapped to the side on impact and Mary froze as her hand dropped to her side. His face stayed facing away from her, he flexed his jaw as a series of small blisters bubbled on his cheek, like he'd been burned. She saw a drop of blood trickle from his lip and down his chin.

Oh shit.

Blind panic doused out her hate fire and she darted between the party-goers, desperate to find an exit. She was always running from Dante it seemed.

Mary bolted, finding the sliding door that led out to the backyard. She ran out into the wide space, checking both sides to see if there was a back gate she could slip out of. A big pool took up most of the yard and she lunged to her left,

Violet E.C

eager to get lost in the few groups out here and then find an exit. But not before a rough hand grabbed the back of her shirt, lifting her off her feet.

She struggled and kicked, flinging her legs around in an attempt to hit her attacker. He grabbed her shoulder and spun her around to face him, her feet firmly planted on the ground for a split second. His eyes were pure black, Mary couldn't tell where his pupil ended and his iris began. His cheek was still blistered, looking raw and painful. Mary frowned, suddenly confused, but didn't dwell on it as her heart thumped in her chest in fear.

Dante's lip was slightly swollen and split, dried blood was smeared across it like he'd wiped it with his hand. She felt a little satisfaction at her artwork on his face. He lifted her again by the collar of her shirt, her legs dangling helplessly and he looked her dead in the eye.

"Sink or swim."

And with that, he pushed her chest, letting go of her collar, and Mary stumbled back into the freezing, chlorinated water. The cold initially shocked her, knocking the air out of her lungs, but what made her panic more was the sudden weight holding her shoulders down.

Mary kicked and squirmed as she tried to break free of Dante's iron grip on her. She panicked, her feet not able to touch the bottom of the pool. She opened her mouth to scream, but inhaled a mouthful of cold water instead. Her body tried to force her to cough it up but she couldn't, her mouth still open in a noiseless scream.

Her lungs burned and constricted, empty of any air and her legs ached from kicking so hard. Her heartbeat roared in her ears, a thunderous rhythm that added to her panic. Her limbs felt full of lead weights and her movements became sluggish. Mary saw silhouettes above the water, muffled voices mixed in

Inferno

with the bass thumping in her skull.

This is it, she thought blurrily, her mind deprived of oxygen. *This is when I die, and it'll all be because of Dante Enfer.*

Black spots clouded her vision as she feebly tried to wrestle free, but Dante's grip was too strong, his weight too heavy for her to shift off.

Just as she thought she'd drown there, in some random teenager's pool in the middle of a house party, Dante's hold on her was released and she floated to the surface, barely coherent, as her brain began to shut down.

She noticed splashing around her and a few hands yanked her out, rolling her onto her side at the pool's edge. Someone smacked her hard on the back and the pool water forced its way up her throat and out.

She coughed and spluttered, her lungs heaving as if she'd swallowed up the whole pool. Her body convulsed and she gulped up the air greedily, not caring if it stank of cigarettes and alcohol. A few of her classmates surrounded her and Mary glanced around the yard, trying to spot Dante. He was nowhere to be seen and she swore under her breath.

"Maz, are you okay?" Ally's voice invaded her thoughts and she turned to see her best friend soaked in pool water too, gripping Mary's hand like a vice. Mark was next to her, his dark hair dripping wet and a few others crouched around her, concerned looks on their faces.

Mary couldn't answer; her throat hurt, tears stung in her eyes along with her smudged makeup. She knew her white shirt was probably see-through and her hair matted and stringy. She shivered, the pool water had been freezing, and outside was no better.

Embarrassment flamed on her face that half of this party had witnessed her near drowning and all at the hands of the Devil himself.

Violet E.C

Someone handed her a bottle of water and she took it, whispering a small "thank you" with a hoarse voice. Ally stood up and cleared the concerned party goers, announcing that Mary would be fine.

Mary was thankful, she hated attention at the best of times and this most definitely was not her finest hour. Ally sat back down next to her, smoothing Mary's wet hair off her face in a motherly way. She glanced at her best friend, seeing her eyes slightly bloodshot and her pupils were wide.

Even though Mary and Ally were best friends, they were far from similar. Ally's wardrobe consisted of black everything, socks and underwear included. Her hair was naturally black, and she always sported thick eyeliner that flicked up at the corners of her eyes, complimenting her East Asian features.

Ally's mom didn't approve of her lifestyle or her fashion. It was always a point of contention at home when Mary went over, so Ally often stayed at Mark's.

Although Mary didn't really like Mark, he never did wrong by Ally. He treated her well, was loyal, and most of all, he made her happy. Plus he had just helped rescue her from Dante's death mission, so he was in her good books for now.

"What happened?" Mary whispered and Ally glanced at Mark briefly. A look was shared between the two of them, but she was too tired to try and figure out what it meant.

"We heard splashing and assumed someone had got in the pool, even though Jesse told everyone to stay out of it because it's being cleaned tomorrow."

Great, so not only had Dante tried to drown her, but she'd probably swallowed enough algae and God knows what chemicals to die later.

"Then we came outside for a smoke and saw Dante holding someone down in the pool, when we got closer, I saw your hair and I just freaked, Maz. I started yelling at Dante, Mark pushed him off, told him it wasn't funny. I jumped in, trying to swim to you and Mark did too. Once we got you out, your lips were blue and for a second, oh God, I thought you were dead." Ally sniffed and Mary squeezed her hand. It was funny how Mary was comforting Ally when she was the one who'd been nearly drowned.

Mary nodded, the story clearer in her head. She shivered in her wet clothes, feeling like death. Ally grabbed a random hoodie from a nearby chair and wrapped it around Mary's shoulders. It reeked of some teenager's cheap cologne, but Mary didn't care. Grateful, her now pink lips pulled into the tiniest of smiles.

"Let's get you home," Mark said, placing Mary's arm around his neck and the other around Ally's. They both stood up, carrying her between them, Mary's feet barely touching the ground as they made their way back to his car.

As they slid her into the backseat, Mary's eyelids felt heavy, as if someone was pushing them shut. Sleep felt like an old friend and she let her head fall back on the seat. In the front, Mark and Ally spoke in hushed voices.

"What are you guys talking about?" Mary murmured, eyes still shut. They were silent for a moment, then Mark gunned the engine and the car started to move. Sleep welcomed her with open arms as she fell into oblivion.

Chapter Five: Tension

Present Day

As he ordered at the counter of the small deli, Mary didn't take her eyes off him for one moment. She had so many questions burning in her mind:

Why was he back?

What did he want with her?

Why was he working at the exact same firm as her?

It was not a coincidence, *definitely not.* Mary didn't believe in that.

He sauntered over to her table, grinning smugly as he sat down on the chair opposite her. He seemed too big for it, his broad chest and wide shoulders looking comical on the small plastic chair. He studied her for a moment, openly staring Mary down and she refused to look away although his dark eyes burned into her own and made her want to squirm under his hot gaze. The tension was palpable, thick in the air as they watched each other.

He was dressed in his usual leather jacket, his glasses pushed back on his head, dark strands escaped, and dangled over his forehead. Mary noticed every female head, and some male ones too, turning in their direction.

God, why did you put me on Earth with this insufferable hunk of a man?

Unwrapping his sandwich, he kept his smug grin. It irritated Mary and without a second thought, the question just popped out.

"Why did you lie to Monica?"

Okay, not the exact question Mary intended to ask, there were about a thousand different, probably more important ones, but this one was burning on her tongue.

Dante's eyebrows rose, obviously not expecting her to ask that particular question either. He hesitated, wondering whether she was onto him and his plan. Deciding that she wasn't suspicious enough yet, he assumed she was asking about him mentioning their history.

"I didn't lie. I said we hung out a lot."

"No, we didn't," Mary argued, jaw locked and nostrils flared. Dante irritated every fiber in her being and she couldn't stand him. Regardless of his good looks, he was still an asshole and she hadn't forgotten what he'd done ten years ago.

"Well, we did. We saw each other every day and we spent time around each other." He smirked, like he had an internal joke that only he knew about. "I never said we liked each other."

Mary opened her mouth to argue but snapped it shut. *Damn it, he's right.* He didn't technically lie, but she also wouldn't call Dante's daily harassment "hanging out".

"Where did you go?" Mary still stared hard at Dante, she didn't even know if she was blinking at all. Her questions just rolled off her tongue without her brain even registering them.

"I'm right here."

Violet E.C

"That's not what I asked." Mary frowned and Dante sat back, seemingly unfazed by her interrogation over sandwiches.

"Well, that's what I answered."

Resisting the urge to slam his head into the table, Mary clenched her jaw even harder and let a harsh breath out through her nose. He was infuriating, dodging her questions and generally just being an asshole.

Dante studied her from across the small table, he'd devoured his sandwich in practically 1.5 seconds so he stretched his arms up and laced his fingers together at the back of his head. His large biceps flexed and Mary had to focus very hard on just looking at his face.

He watched her, as tense as anything, with her barely touched sandwich as she exhaled a particularly loud breath. He almost laughed as she struggled to keep her composure.

"Feeling frustrated? I can help with that." He smirked.

Mary clenched her jaw so hard, she thought she'd crack a tooth. He was such a pain in the ass.

"Am I getting under your skin?" His tone was seductive but also mocking and Mary once again envisioned smacking his head into the table. *It would make the most satisfying cracking sound, I'm sure.*

Her mouth set in a hard line as she stared right back. What was once fear, Mary realized, was now anger. Dante had messed up her high school life, he'd publicly humiliated her, tried to drown her amongst many other things. Mary had never stood up for herself at school, but she'd grown a backbone in the last ten years and she planned on using it.

"You have an overinflated opinion of your importance in my life." She crossed her arms over her chest and feigned disinterest as she stared him down.

Dante's eyebrows rose again, *was that admiration in his eyes?* She questioned. It was gone in a flash and replaced with a

Inferno

challenging look. Mary swallowed down the fear that tried to bubble in her throat. No, she would not be intimidated or bullied again. And certainly not by Dante Enfer.

"Oh Mary Mack, you have no idea how much I fit into your life. Since I've uprooted my life to find you, I think I'll be sticking around."

This time, Mary couldn't help her jaw falling slack at Dante's admission. What was so important about her that he'd completely uproot his life for her? Was he obsessed with her? Maybe he was a stalker?

"I'm only gonna say this once Dante, so listen up." Mary leaned in and Dante's intrigued eyes met hers. He bent forward too, getting up close to her. She felt that nervousness, that jittery feeling in her body when her eyes met his. She filed that away for future thought once she had some time alone to get her head together after today's train wreck.

"I don't care what obsession you have with me. But I'm not the scared little girl you liked to pick on in high school. I left her behind in Neverfield and guess what? She's not coming back, so you can forget anything you thought you knew about me because the old Mary is dead. This Mary has thicker skin and she will fight back. Got it?"

Mary rose and Dante stood up too, towering over her at the table. He braced his arms on the tabletop, leaning down to get to her level and looking her straight in the eye.

She swallowed her fear again, gosh, why was she so jittery? Her hands shook, whether from adrenaline from standing up to her childhood bully or something else, she couldn't decipher and her brain was scattered.

He smelt like cigarettes and musk again and her heart started a new, faster beat. Mary willed it to shut up even though she was positive Dante couldn't hear it.

He grinned, clearly hearing her fast-paced heartbeat, seeing

Violet E.C

her shaking hands, and knowing exactly what effect he had on her. He admired her spunk, but also the way she was leaning over the table, so her shirt was falling open, tempting him with her full chest underneath. His hands itched to touch her, tease her, have her begging for him. His dick twitched in his pants and he had to refrain from taking her there and then on the crappy plastic table in the middle of the bustling deli.

"Oh, I hear you Mary Mack. But you see, you can change your hair, your clothes, your eye color, but you can't change what's on the inside and that scared little girl? She's never going away. You can pretend you're being brave, but I still see that little girl. So you listen to me, Mary. I'm here in your life and I'm back to make it living Hell, baby. So hop on and enjoy the ride. Because I know you will."

And with that, he winked- actually winked!- and strode away. Mary stared after him, her composure dissolved as she shakily sat down once he'd left the cafe. She'd had everything locked away, every part of her life back home was safely stored under lock and key in her brain.

All those feelings, emotions, and memories stored were safely away and just like that, Dante brought them all rushing back to the surface, overwhelming her. She was angry, frustrated and although she'd never admit it openly, she was turned on. Her fight was Dante had left her hot and bothered in more ways than one.

He'd noticed her hair color, well, that wasn't exactly hard to notice, Mary's platinum white-blonde hair was now a dark brown, courtesy of a box dye in her first night in the city that she kept up every month. She'd been convinced that a new look- a new identity was what she needed to succeed and it had worked. Until Dante came in and smashed all her walls down with one conversation.

Her eyes. Yes, of course, he'd pointed out her eyes. The new

Inferno

Mary bought blue contacts to cover up her silver eyes and walked down the sidewalk with her head held high because she was confident and strong. Not weak and unique. And that was what she believed.

Until today.

～

Taking a very deep breath, or five, Mary pushed down the handle and entered what was her office, and was now a joint space with Dante. If she thought God hated her before, she really believed he despised her now.

A small desk had been added to the side of the room, facing the window and looking out over the large city. From up here, people looked like toys, so small and insignificant that Mary often stared down, watching people go about their lives, each one a unique story. It fascinated her.

And there he sat at his desk, again looking too big for it. He wore just his black shirt, rolled up at the elbows to expose his tattooed forearms. *That's hot*, the thought popped into her head before she could stop it. She shook her head, *no, don't think like that.*

Mary briefly flicked back in her memories to see if she ever noticed his tattoos in high school, she couldn't remember ever seeing him without his jacket so she didn't know.

His form was hunched over a laptop as he typed away, pretending he couldn't see her just standing in the doorway, looking like she was surveying the room, but secretly checking him out. Knowing she was staring made him smirk, he'd got under her skin.

"Are you going to gawk at me all day or do you actually do work here?"

Mary snapped out of her daze, cursing herself and Dante in the same sentence in her head, and slid behind her desk, settling down to an afternoon of work. Her spa day plans were a distant memory at this point and she sighed.

Opening her laptop, she resisted the temptation to glance over at Dante, but she was curious as to what he was doing. Perhaps Monica had set some work for him to do, just easy stuff like property searching or collecting names for potential sellers and buyers.

"I can feel your fake ocean eyes staring at the back of my head, Mother Mary."

Gritting her teeth, Mary's eyes snapped back to her laptop and she tried to read an email from a client but she kept going over and over the same line, not absorbing anything.

The minutes dragged by and after fifteen of them, Mary knew working with Dante in her office was not going to happen. She had to get this induction shit over and done with, and fast, so she could get him out of her office and her hair.

Somewhere, deep down she knew it wasn't going to be that easy. Hadn't Dante said that he was back to make her life "living Hell" after all? Shaking those thoughts away, Mary picked up her phone and dialed a client she'd been meaning to get in touch with.

Dante's head twisted as he heard her talk down the phone, his ears zoning into the conversation. She'd swiveled her chair around so he couldn't see her face but Dante still stared, intrigued by how this grown up, sophisticated woman could be the shy, nervous girl who he pestered at school. He liked her fire, her change of pace but he knew the old Mary was still in there, and he was determined to get her out again. Her fear did things to him that he'd very openly admit because he was a cocky bastard.

Mary ended the call and he snapped out of his thoughts.

"Right, we're going to go and view a property so you can see what kind of stuff we sell and list. As you've probably guessed, we're not any average brokerage, we deal in luxury property which means good manners and big money, one of which you might need to work on."

"Your tone's pretty daring Mary Mack, considering you all but fainted earlier when I told you why I was here. Did you have to change your panties after our little chat?" He smirked.

Mary stared back at him, no emotion showing on her face. Dante thought he'd score on that one, but Mary seemed harder to crack than before. Lucky for him, he loved a good challenge.

"Grab your jacket, we'll get a taxi to the property. The owner is going to meet us there."

She stood, picking up her bag and coat, and strode out to the door, not giving him a second glance. Dante's eyebrows rose as he shrugged on his jacket and followed Mary out into the hallway.

What he didn't know, was that Mary's body was set alight by his words and she was even more infuriated that he knew how turned on she was by him. She needed her body to stop being such a hopeless romantic. Not that there was any romance involved when it came to Dante.

The taxi ride was silent, his leg was a mere breath from Mary's and she all but threw herself out of the car, opting to cross her legs and press herself against the door as much as possible to avoid any contact when the car turned a corner. Dante, who was never one for pretenses, enjoyed watching Mary squirm in the car, avoiding any inch of contact with him; it was very entertaining. He spread his legs wider, making her squash her body into the door even more. He chuckled under his breath as she avoided his touch like the plague.

The property wasn't far from her office and she was relieved when the car pulled up and the owner- a short man with grey hair- was waiting outside.

Violet E.C

"Mary, it's so good to hear from you. I wondered when you wanted to view the property." He shook her hand fondly and Mary smiled back at him and fell into easy conversation. Dante held back, watching the scene unfold before him. Mary had been nothing but hostile to him since he arrived, not that he could blame her, but it was interesting to see this side of her.

"I'm going to have to leave you as I have to run off, but here are the keys," he placed a set of keys in Mary's palm. "I'll stop by the office to pick them up tomorrow."

Mary shook his hand again, smiling and he hailed a cab, briefly glancing at Dante but not saying anything. He had that effect on people.

"Well, I guess the place is ours then," Dante said, looking up at the elegant skyrise.

Mary said nothing but gripped the keys harder so they dug into her palm painfully and made her way to the door.

Dante followed in suit, stopping just behind her as he got to the entrance. Although she'd dyed her hair dark, some white strands still glinted in the sunshine. It was pulled into a tight bun at the nape of her neck and he thought about her neck, how it would feel to hold it in his grip, to run his fingers down it. To run his tongue along her soft skin and how she'd moan his name...

The click of the key in the lock brought Dante out of his thoughts and he groaned mentally, thinking about the ways he could mark her perfect skin.

Mary led the way in, opting for the stairs rather than the elevator. She did not want to be in a small space with Dante again, the taxi journey alone had been enough.

He walked behind her, keeping his distance for now. The building was expensive, marble pillars decorated the lobby and the staircase banister was so shiny that Mary could see

Inferno

Dante's reflection in it as he watched her every move.

They climbed one set of stairs and Mary opened the second door on the left. She walked in before him, leaving the door open behind her. She dropped her bag and coat on the counter and her eyes widened at the sight in front of her. Of course, she'd seen her fair share of beautiful properties that she was able to sell and get good commission on, but this one really was a dream.

The usual properties were furnished in bland neutral colors but here, the owner had gone for warm tones, with woodwork and cream furnishings. It was truly her dream home. The balcony overlooked the luscious private gardens below and Mary stood out there, gazing at everything she wanted. A slice of heaven in the middle of the chaotic city.

Dante leaned his shoulder against the frame of the balcony doors, crossing his arms over his broad chest as he observed from behind her, noting the way she sighed deeply and how all the tension seemed to leave her body. The sun streamed in, bathing the balcony in a warm glow and for a moment, Dante's breath was taken away by her sheer beauty.

He stared at the curves of her body as he imagined her writhing under him. His head was in the gutter today but he didn't even care, she tempted him in a way he'd never felt before. It was more than lust, it was a primal need. It always had been, ever since the first time he'd seen her in high school. He loved being around her, antagonizing her, tearing her down.

As Mary looked out to the garden, she felt him behind her, pressed into her, thighs to thighs and his chest to her back. Her short moment of inner peace rapidly dissolved and was replaced by panic, mixed with lust. Her heartbeat sped up, her body equally loved and hated having him so close. He clouded her every thought. She needed space, but she knew he wouldn't ever listen to her, so she did the next best thing and lifted an elbow to ram into his chest to knock him back.

Dante dodged her attempt and grabbed her arms, holding them by her wrists behind her back, at the base of her spine. His large hand detained them, his fingers brushing dangerously close to her ass and sending a spike of electricity up her back. His other hand grabbed her hips roughly. Her chest arched upwards as he bent her back towards him. Mary's breath came out in short gasps and he leaned close to her ear.

"Tsk tsk Mary Mack, violence isn't very nice, now is it?" His hot breath tickled her skin, spreading goosebumps in its wake and she felt a flush crawling up her chest.

"I seem to remember that's all you resorted to back in high school." She spat out through gritted teeth. Mary wriggled to break Dante's hold but he was stronger, gripping her wrists so tightly she was sure she'd bruise. She hated how much this reminded her of high school, of how Dante would have such a tight grip on her and she detested how much her body liked it.

"That was my game when I was eighteen, I know better now." His lips ghosted over her neck and for a moment Mary didn't know whether to gasp in shock or joy. Pleasure rippled through her and she tried to chide herself for getting caught up in this fantasy. But the feeling of his hot lips on her neck erased any rational thought in her brain.

Dante trailed his mouth up to the shell of her ear and very gently licked it. Mary jerked, the feeling of his hot, wet tongue against her skin felt sinful. She squeezed her thighs together, slickness pooling between her legs. She bit her lip and clenched her jaw as she suppressed the ache in her lower belly.

Mary pushed her ass into him, feeling his hard-on poking into her lower back. She groaned quietly. Her skin tingled, her wrists hurt and her body began to ache for release as Dante continued to tease her with his tongue. He smelt like

Inferno

smoke, heavy and musky and she realized with a start, that she liked the smell.

As Mary squirmed in his arms, Dante realized how easy this could be for him. She was already putty in his hands; her chest rose and fell rapidly and he could hear her heartbeat thumping double-time as he caressed her milky skin. She smelled divine, a sweet and floral scent mixed with her natural smell made him almost groan out loud. He couldn't see her face as her back was to him, but he knew her cheeks would be flushed bright red.

He'd thought this would be an emotionless game, but suddenly the feelings from ten years ago rushed to the surface, the moment when Mary'd hit him at Jesse's party and he'd almost drowned her for it. Their anger, her glow, his lust.

He wanted to make her pay, he knew what he was here for, but then again, messing around with her head was another way to ruin her. Maybe if he fucked her, he'd get this weird feeling out of his system. There was no denying their attraction, but it was just lust after all.

Dante's teeth grazed over Mary's neck as he pushed her chin to face him with his other hand. He caught sight of her beautiful profile. He stared at her full lips, again finding himself wondering what they'd taste like, how they'd feel. Mary was tough but he knew her weaknesses and he wondered if she'd resist him. Would she give in to this moment or would she fight him with every fiber of her being?

Whilst he contemplated, Mary stood before him, eyes closed, lips parted and her neck flushed. Suddenly he had this desperate need to see her eyes. To remember the exact shade of silver with golden flecks and how they glowed when she got mad.

"Open your eyes."

They snapped open, but the unfamiliar shade of blue was

jarring and the trance was quickly shattered as they both broke free from the spell they were under. Mary'd got caught up in her feelings. Just the feeling of having someone touch her, someone caress her. God, she needed to get laid soon. Not Dante though, *never* Dante.

Without a second thought for what she just let him do to her and how much she enjoyed it, Mary threw her head back and it connected with a satisfying crunch with his chin. Dante released her hands out of shock as he felt blood rush into his mouth. He'd bitten his fucking tongue. Anger flared inside of him as he pushed aside the lust he'd felt for Mary in his arms.

Spitting the blood out, he stepped forward. Mary had spun around now and he caged her in with his arms. She stared him down, any hint of the desire she previously felt was erased from her face as she clenched her jaw, ready to throw a punch if needed. Her neck and chest were still rosy red and flushed, she hated that he'd got her riled up so easily. She wasn't afraid as he towered over her, blocking the sunlight so his body became a silhouette, his face in shadow. His black eyes were even darker and she knew that look all too well.

Dante lowered his face to hers. She knew this technique, he was always trying to intimidate her using his physical size and presence. But she wouldn't be scared that easily.

"Get out of my face." She growled before shoving his arm away. His grip remained strong and he stared at her.

Ducking quickly, Mary managed to get out from under his arm and darted inside. She rushed to the front door, her heels clicking on the wood floors.

A hand grabbed her wrist and spun her around, pushing her back up against the wall next to the door. Their bodies were flush, her skin itched with the longing that she'd felt not so long ago. The tingles were still there, begging for release.

Inferno

Mary glanced over Dante's shoulder, seeing her purse on the counter top. If she could reach it then she could call Monica, report Dante's shitty behavior and be rid of him. A little voice inside her head told her it wouldn't be that easy, but she blocked it out along with the one that said she loved having Dante's hands on her. They were traitorous little voices and she didn't need them.

"Looking for this?" Dante reached into his pocket, her phone was in his hand and he smirked as he leaned forward, his face in line with hers and raised his fist, smashing her phone against the wall, a few inches away from her head.

It took everything in her not to flinch and look away from his eyes as the glass and plastic pieces fell to the floor beside her. Mary swallowed, her resolve slowly crumbling as Dante's eyes glinted. He pushed his body further into hers, and she kept her face impassive as she felt his hard cock pressing into her stomach. Her heartbeat thundered in her ears, half due to fear and half to a part of her that she didn't want to fully acknowledge yet. Her thighs squeezed together involuntarily, her lower belly still clenching.

"What do you want with me?"

Dante smirked, his lips spreading into a nasty grin.

"I told you earlier Mary Mack, I'm here to make you regret the day you crossed me."

"Stay away from me," Mary growled, her skin glowed again and she tried to calm down, noticing her hands emitting a faint light. *Not again.*

"Challenge accepted." Dante grinned, dropping a not-so-friendly kiss on her forehead and folding his arms over his chest. Her skin was hot and almost blistering under his lips.

"Lead the way then." His eyes glinted as he gestured at the door. Mary pushed off from the wall, straightened her dress, and grabbed her purse off the counter, minus her phone. She glanced at the crumbled pieces on the floor and internally sighed.

It was going to be a long day.

Chapter Six: The Vicar

Ten Years Ago

The clock ticked obnoxiously loudly in the principal's waiting room as Mary and her dad sat on two chairs next to each other in silence.

Ally had dropped her off last night and much to Mary's dismay, she'd gone to get her dad to carry her from the car. Of course, he had freaked out too, taken her to the hospital where she'd been discharged after a checkup, but he'd insisted that they report Dante's behavior to the principal first thing in the morning.

Mary had been reluctant to confess who had been responsible for her attempted drowning, not because she wanted to protect Dante, she couldn't care less about the bully, but because she feared what else he'd do to her.

After an hour of persuading her to open up, Alan had finally got his answer and God knew how angry he had been. But he kept a lid on it for Mary's benefit, rather than marching straight over to Dante's house and beating him black and blue for even considering harming a hair on his daughter's head.

"Mr. Lux, Mary, please come in."

It was Sunday morning, her dad had made her get up before they were due at church and drive to school to speak to the principal.

"I understand this is a matter of importance as it is a Sunday," he spoke sharply, eyeing both Mary and her dad and putting emphasis on his final word. "So let's get down to it, shall we?"

Principal Mathers was a friendly enough man, but Mary never really felt that he liked kids or even liked his job. Maybe he just did his job for the paycheck. Alan hoped he'd care enough to keep his daughter safe when she was out of his sight.

"Well, last night there was an incident between Mary and one of your students; Dante Enfer. I've heard he's a troublemaker, but last night he tried to drown Mary in someone's pool at a party." Her dad's fists shook as he barely contained his anger and Mary put a hand over his comfortingly.

"I see. I'm sorry to hear that Mr. Lux. How are you, Mary?" Principal Mathers turned to her and she shrugged.

"Okay, I guess-"

"How would you feel after being nearly drowned, Principal Mathers?" Her dad snapped, eyes hard.

The principal's mouth opened and closed like a fish gasping for water. He was obviously not used to being talked to like that. Mary subtly smirked at the principal's lack of words, she kind of liked seeing him being put in his place and by none other than her dad.

"Dante is a menace and he must be dealt with accordingly."

"Yes, yes of course Mr. Lux, we will take the appropriate course of action for Mr. Enfer, but we will need to ask other students, gather witnesses before we can do anything about

Inferno

his behavior."

"We need this sorted now Principal Mathers, I will not have my daughter in a school where one of the students tried to kill her!"

Mary had never seen her dad so worked up, sweat beaded his brow and he was particularly red in the face.

"Dad." She gently said a small reassuring smile appeared on her face.

"I'll be okay. I'm sure Principal Mathers will get this under control, but for now, I'll be careful."

Her dad looked at her for a long moment before sighing.

"I apologize for my outburst." He said and rubbed his hands on his tired face.

The principal nodded and her dad rose from his chair, straightening his tie.

"I can assure, you Mr. Lux, we will deal with this properly and effectively. Your daughter will be safe in our hands."

"I would hope so."

～

"I need to get to the church for the Sunday sermon, you don't have to come if you don't want to though." Her dad said as they got out of the car at their house.

"Okay," Mary said quietly, pulling her jacket tighter around her body, protecting herself from the winter chill and the unease from Dante's attack that settled in the pit of her stomach. She needed time in to think, to talk to someone who wouldn't judge. "I think I'll go and visit Mom."

Her dad stiffened for a moment, then nodded as he watched his daughter walk in the direction of the church.

Alan stood watching her retreating form- a spitting image of his late wife- for a moment before going inside. He took a deep breath and walked in the direction of his study.

Violet E.C

Books were scattered over every surface, some closed and some open with old, yellowing pages and faded drawings. Alan stepped over the stack of books on the floor by his desk and picked one up that he'd left open.

Alan flicked through the pages, finding one with a torn square of paper slotted in the spine. A number was written in spidery handwriting on the scrap. Reaching for the phone on his desk, he dialed the number and waited.

"Good morning, my name is Pastor Lux, from Neverfield. Can I speak with The Vicar?"

There was a muffled answer at the end of the line and Alan gently pushed his glasses up the bridge of his nose, tapping his fingers on the desk as he listened.

"Well, you see there's someone in my town, a nuisance and possibly of the other kind."

The person on the other end interrupted and Alan held his breath, his tapping ceased and his brow creased.

"No, I mean from *below*." His voice was barely above a whisper, although his house was empty as Mary was out.

He nodded, listening intently to the caller, answering 'yes' and 'no' in intervals. After a short moment, the call ended and Alan replaced the phone in the cradle, before sitting down in his chair and looking out of the window into the yard.

His search for the Book of Aeternum had proved fruitless thus far, after asking all of the neighboring towns' pastors, none of them had heard anything about the book for years, even decades. Even the Mayor and the Sheriff hadn't heard anything, though there had been a few laughs at Alan's expense.

It had been quiet since the passing of Eve, their town lay undisturbed by anything otherworldly and Alan felt unsettled. It was like a storm waiting to break. He worried about the book and whether it had fallen into the wrong hands. He was

Inferno

constantly fretting about Mary and keeping her safe, making sure she never knew of the dangers outside their front door which shouldn't even be on this Earth.

And now Dante Enfer was someone he had to sort out. He'd heard the name around town; the boy with no parents, who lived in the house on the hill by himself. The townspeople had spread vicious rumors about his parents, who they were, what happened to them. Some said drug dealers, others said child traffickers. Whatever the story was, Dante had piqued Alan's interest early on, and not in a good way.

Then, with the events of last night; an attempted drowning with none other than his only daughter, Alan knew he needed this sorted out and fast. He suspected Dante to be from below, he just wasn't sure. Either way, he needed that boy gone.

Sighing, he checked the clock on his mantelpiece and pushed himself out of the chair, weaving around the stacks of books and picking up his Bible from its usual spot.

Alan glanced at a framed picture of him and his wife, smiling and holding baby Mary in their arms. Eve's glow was faint, missable unless you knew what you were looking for. But he saw it in Mary every day. Not only did she grow to look like her mother with every breathing moment, but she had the traits. They weren't sure if she'd inherit her mother's abilities, there was a 50/50 chance after all, but Alan knew the signs and he knew what they meant too.

~

Taking a tentative step into her first class on Monday morning, Mary tried to calm her nerves. She gripped her backpack straps to try to occupy her shaking hands. She shared first-period Biology with Dante and she dreaded what he was planning after his failed attempt at murder on Saturday. She hadn't eaten any breakfast, too worried about what he had in mind for her and she felt sick to the stomach because of it.

She scanned the class, finding a seat relatively close to the back, next to some kid that she barely ever talked to. After another glance at the room, she noted that Ally was absent again and made a mental note to check in with her after school.

Setting her bag down, she tucked herself into the chair at the back corner and sighed, not ready for another long day. With any luck, Dante wouldn't be in and Mary could relax and not have to panic every time someone walked into the classroom.

But luck was not on her side today.

As she looked up to check the clock by the door, a tall, broad, dark-haired figure strode in and she resisted darting out of the room or hiding in a storage closet. Dante's eyes automatically found hers and he grinned before making his way down the aisle to her desk. His face was healed, with no signs of any of the damage that Mary had caused on the weekend.

"Move."

The kid next to her all but squealed as he scooped up his books and scurried over to the next desk. Dante slid into the seat next to Mary and she scooted her chair even further away so she was practically sitting on the edge of the table.

"Come on, that's no way to treat a friend."

We're not friends, Mary thought to herself but didn't dare voice it. She swallowed hard and faced forward, pretending to ignore what Dante said.

"Don't be shy, now Mary Mack." He reached over and tugged her chair with no effort, it scraped across the Lino floors, and soon it was back next to his with less than a breath between them.

The scent of leather mixed with cigarettes and aftershave assaulted her senses and Mary saw him smirk in her peripher-

Inferno

al vision as she kept her eyes on the board.

Silently praying the teacher would arrive any second, Mary gulped and tried to stay stock still as Dante watched her. She could have almost been a mannequin with her glass skin and perfect hair, but Mary's constant fidgeting and rapid breathing gave her away.

He leaned in close, close enough to smell her freshly washed white locks and he inhaled lightly. She smelled good; floral and sweet with a slight hint of chlorine. He smiled smugly at the reminder of what he'd attempted on Saturday night.

"Did you have a nice swim on the weekend, Mary Mack?" He spoke quietly, so no one else around could hear him.

She froze next to him, her heartbeat increased and Dante could hear her sharp intake of breath. Her reaction was exactly what he was looking for, she was riled up and he loved it.

"Next time you get in a pool, it'll be your last."

Mary's heart stopped at the very obvious threat that hung in the air. She thought she might faint and she looked around the room, only moving her eyes to see if anyone else had noticed. All the students were chatting amongst themselves, oblivious to the horrific threat that Dante just posed. The blood drained from her cheeks and she wondered if she'd puke.

"Why me?" She whispered, barely audible and her voice cracked. Dante heard her and grinned, opening his mouth to reply.

Before he could answer, the teacher strolled in and announced silence as the bell rang. Still watching Mary, Dante ignored the rest of the class, focused on how his threat had fazed her. How her heart beat irregularly and how sweat beaded on her skin. He wondered, hoped even that she'd faint. Any excuse to get her out of the classroom so he can have his way with her. He'd finish her off this time.

Violet E.C

A kid from another class ran in through the still-open door and passed a note to the teacher. He opened it and looked around the room.

"Mr. Enfer and Miss Lux, you're wanted in the principal's office."

Mary nodded, reaching down to pick up her backpack with shaky hands. She swallowed hard and slung it over her shoulder as she slinked out of the classroom. Dante followed in suit, grinning widely at Jesse who reached out for a fist bump.

Once they reached the Principal's office, Mary took a deep breath and knocked on the door.

Principal Mathers opened the door with a tight smile and gestured for them to sit in the chairs opposite his desk.

Settling down behind his desk, he looked at both of the students, assessing the moment before speaking.

"It's been brought to my attention that you caused quite some harm to Mary this weekend, Dante."

Mary watched Dante as he leaned back in his chair, linking his fingers behind his head, and looked at the principal blankly.

Realizing that he wasn't going to get an easy confession or an apology, Principal Mathers quickly continued.

"With the recent events of the weekend and many student stories to back it up, I'm afraid that your actions have caused some serious consequences. And because of that, I'm going to have to ask you to leave the school."

Mary's mouth involuntarily popped open, surprise painted on her features. She had expected something, but not expulsion. Okay, well Dante *had* tried to drown her, that was pretty bad.

The tense silence dragged out as Dante's eyes hardened and Principal Mathers adjusted his tie, fidgeting and looking uncomfortable under Dante's searing gaze.

Inferno

"At this time, you're lucky the police haven't been involved, but we'd prefer to keep it that way. This school has a great track record and I don't want to taint that."

Glaring hotly, Dante cocked his head slightly, almost challenging the principal, and a bead of sweat formed on his brow, dripping down his face as he avoided eye contact with the boy in front of him.

"Gosh, it's hot in here, isn't it?" He rambled on.

He stood up and opened the window whilst fanning himself, sweat was now running tracks down his face, darkening his starched collar. Mary stared in disbelief. It couldn't be Dante causing the principal to sweat like that, could it? She could feel an electrical buzz in the air, it was heavy, like the air before a storm.

"We'll give you references for another school and you can finish early today." He avoided eye contact and Dante stood, suddenly feeling the hot anger bubbling up inside him like a volcano. He turned to Mary and she visibly cringed as his fully black eyes felt like they scorched her fair skin.

"This isn't over." He motioned between the two of them and ripped open the door with so much force that it rocked on its hinges, threatening to fall off. The secretary on the other side gasped as Dante stormed out, visible smoke coming off his skin. Mary blinked, wondering if she was seeing things. The room smelled faintly of burning and she frowned.

"Off to class please, Miss Lux."

Principal Mathers was still looking out of the window and watched Dante thunder across the parking lot. He turned and made eye contact with the principal, grinning sinisterly before stretching his legs over the body of his motorcycle and kicking off, revving the engine purposefully loudly as he burned his tires before speeding away leaving nothing but a cloud of smoke and the stench of singed rubber.

Violet E.C

Mary, having witnessed the whole thing, swallowed thickly, her mouth feeling dry and her head was spinning, the lingering smell making her feel sick and dizzy.

"May I be excused for the rest of the day, sir? I can catch up on work tomorrow and after class."

Without looking at her, the principal nodded and Mary walked slowly out of the office before the world faded to black and she faintly heard another gasp before hitting the floor.

∼

Dante slammed the front door and stormed into the living room, he threw himself down on the couch, it cracked under his weight. He was too angry to be concerned, his skin burned so hotly that he ripped off his jacket and t-shirt in one, revealing his chiseled torso and the tattoos that scattered his lean body.

They weren't designs though. Usually, kids his age that had ink had a "hard" design like a skull or a snake. His were swirls, patterns unreadable to the human eye but to Dante- who'd inked them on himself- they were spells.

He kicked his feet up on the couch and seethed whilst pulling a cigarette out of his jacket pocket on the floor. He held the smoke between his teeth and clicked his fingers, a flame appearing on his forefinger. He lit it and shook his hand to put out the flame, letting himself relax as the nicotine worked its way around his system.

"Get your boots off the couch!"

Dante heard a yell from the kitchen and looked up to see Ashja; a tall, lean demon with blue skin and purple feathers with her hands on her hips, glaring at him. She stood in the doorway of the living room, her bright blue tail made up of long feathers, swished behind her.

Inferno

"Ashja, why do you even care?" Dante asked, blowing out a puff of smoke as he looked back at the ceiling.

"Because," the demon said, using her tail to clean some dust off a shelf. "You dragged me up here so if we're going to exist in this drab place, we might as well try and make some semblance of a life. Plus your boots leave stains that annoy me." She sighed, exasperated, and narrowed her eyes at him. The smoke coming off his body was visible to the demon's eye.

"You're smoking."

"Thanks." Sarcasm dripped off Dante's voice as he took another puff.

Ashja rolled her eyes and sniffed the air. Some demons emitted a certain smell that only some others could pick up, Dante's smell was angry and charred, almost carcinogenic. She knew he had been royally pissed off today.

"Why are you home early?"

"My plans changed." Dante shrugged, putting his cigarette out on the couch and watching Ashja's brows furrow as she clicked her tongue.

"Well if you actually acted like a human and not a spoiled little devil, then maybe you'd achieve whatever it is that you want up here."

Dante sat up and extended his palm flat out at her, a fireball narrowly missed Ashja's head and singed her head feathers as she ducked with inhuman speed. It fizzled out and left a scorched mark on the dark wood shelf. He wasn't actually aiming for her, but Ashja's nagging wound him up on the best of days, so sometimes he liked to remind her just what he was capable of.

The interior of Dante's house was made up of wine red carpets and dark wood paneling, creating a dim, dark sanctuary for him and Ashja. A magic fire burned all day and all night, making the house painfully hot, replicating Hell's climate,

Violet E.C

and making them feel closer to home.

She huffed and ignored Dante's outburst, brushing her scorched feathers out and letting them fall to the floor, before using her tail to sweep them away into a pile next to the doorway.

"Why you let yourself get riled up by these humans, I'll never know." She said, finding a dustpan and sweeping her fallen feathers into it before emptying it into the trash.

"Because it's more interesting than living in the castle all day."

"Well I liked my job in the castle, and at least the other demons were actually nice to me." She huffed again and walked out of the room.

Lying back on the couch, Dante pondered whether he should go home. He did miss it and his life of luxury in the castle, but he also had no freedom. Here, there were no rules, no one to tell him off and he lived how he wanted to.

Then there was Mary, that infuriating silver-haired girl. She was everything he despised; quiet, shy, faithful and church-going. He had this incessant need to be around her, antagonize her but when he'd tried to kill her, that's when the thrill had really been best. He'd felt almost euphoric. He also felt something else, lust maybe? He wasn't sure, but he wanted to touch her, show her the balance between pain and pleasure. Not that she'd ever let him, that was something he was sure about.

And so now with him being out of school, Dante had to figure out his plan on killing Mary outside of school hours. Of course, he didn't care for the law that these humans laid down so he'd kill her and disappear back home.

Grinning, he began to form a plan in his head, he'd sneak into her house and smother her in the night. No wait, that wasn't as fun, he wanted to see her squirm and plead with those liquid starlight eyes.

Inferno

Having grown up in Hell, Dante had seen many different eye colors, he knew his own were unique, but he'd never seen any like Mary's, not even close. It made him wonder whether she was something else too, something *not human*. Also, the way she glowed, not 100% human either, perhaps she was-

His thought process was interrupted by a crash in the kitchen. He rolled his eyes at the thought of his demon servant breaking something in the house when she was the one who complained about his boot stains. He sat up, listening with his enhanced hearing.

"Ashja?" He called out but he was met with silence. He couldn't even hear her breathing nor the thud of her heartbeat. The hairs on the back of his neck stood up and he instantly knew something was wrong.

Moving too quickly for the human eye, he ran through the kitchen door, eyes scanning the room.

Ashja was slumped on the floor, the top half of her body propped up against the counter and a kitchen knife protruded from the right side of her chest, black liquid oozed from the wound and dripped onto her bright blue feathers. Her head lay to one side and her eyes were wide open and blank, staring into nothingness.

Dante's anger from this morning returned tenfold and smoke poured from every cell in his body. Although Ashja annoyed him, she'd been his companion and housekeeper for the whole time he'd lived on Earth, she was his friend and now she was dead.

Footsteps alerted Dante of an intruder and he stormed out of the kitchen into the hallway, fuming and burning with every step he took.

Spinning around, Dante swiftly avoided the arrow which now was lodged into the wall next to his head. His eyes narrowed as he crept around, using his heightened senses to listen for the intruder. He ducked as another arrow whizzed by, but he wasn't fast enough this time and it buried itself in his bicep. *Fuck, that hurt,* he cursed, anger rapidly boiling inside of him.

Dante let out a roar, rage filling his entire being as he threw a fireball with his good arm. It missed its target, instead setting a curtain on fire. The fire quickly spread and the blaze enveloped the front section of the house. He yanked out the arrow, watching the black blood stain his skin and run down his arm.

"Who are you?" He yelled angrily over the cracking of the fire. Footsteps thudded above him and Dante rushed up the stairs, taking two of them at a time.

A large man, dressed in a black coat and a Fedora hat stood at the other end of the hallway, he had a crossbow in one hand and a silver knife in the other. It glinted orange in the flames. He slowly lifted his head up, revealing his face. It was withered but not old, it had seen many battles with scars and puckered skin. He wore a dog collar around his neck, accompanied by a large silver cross on a chain.

Dante rolled his eyes at the eccentricity of it all. He'd never had much of a taste for theatrics the way humans did.

"I'm The Vicar." The man spoke in a low voice with an accent Dante didn't recognize before dashing forward, his knife pointing at Dante's chest. He darted to his left, managing to block the knife, and rolled into one of the bedrooms. The Vicar was quick on his feet and he slashed the knife upward as Dante threw another fireball, this time setting the rug alight as he tried to dodge the weapon. He sliced the skin on Dante's stomach open in a sideways motion. Black liquid gushed from the wound and Dante growled, putting one hand on his stomach to staunch the bleeding.

The assassin smoothly avoided the fireball, but an ember

caught the hem of his overcoat. He hastily shrugged it off, stamping on it with his heavy boots until it had extinguished. He stood just in a loose shirt and without his coat, Dante noticed he had two more knives sheathed around his waist.

Splaying his palms towards the assassin, Dante let his magic flow freely and let the rage inside him fuel his powers. Fire rushed from his hands, glowing bright orange as it created a burning stream of fire that hit the assassin directly in the stomach.

The Vicar was knocked off his feet by the impact and he flew back into the bookcase, hitting it with a bang and slumping down on the floor beneath it. The knife he was carrying clattered to the floor and Dante kicked it out of arm's reach.

Usually, after using so much power, Dante would be tired, but with the amount of fire and smoke around him, he was energized. Fire was his power and it revitalized him. The arrow wound on his arm and the slash on his stomach was now fully healed.

Still shirtless, the flames in the inferno licked his hot skin, but they didn't burn him. His skin smoldered and The Vicar coughed at the smoke that clogged his airways. There was a gaping hole in his stomach which revealed the books behind him along with his charred organs. Dante stepped over the burning floorboards, a vision in the burning room, immune to the flames, and knelt down next to the assassin.

"Who are you?" He breathed incredulously, staring at this dark angel with flames whipping around him, tattoos shimmering on his sweat-covered skin, dark smoke pouring out from his skin, and a deadly smile painted on his face.

"I'm the Devil." Dante grinned and raised his palm to face the ceiling. The wooden beam above The Vicar creaked before falling and crushing the man below. His heartbeat faded in Dante's ears.

Violet E.C

He stood up and looked around, the house was unsavable and he needed to get out fast. With one fleeting glance at his attempt at a human life, he put his hands together in a praying position and disappeared in a cloud of dark smoke.

Chapter Seven: Secrets

Present Day

Pacing in her condo, Mary debated her next course of action. She could switch her job? Although it wasn't fair nor logical, she just couldn't stay in the office with Dante the Disruptor there.

Frustrated, she ran her hands through her hair and tugged at a knot at the nape of her neck. A few white strands fell out in her fingers and she groaned.

Great, now I'll have to re-dye it again. Just another stress to add to the list, she grumbled. No matter how often Mary dyed her hair, it always seemed to return to its natural color too fast for her to keep up.

Picking up her brand new phone that she bought on the way back from work, she dialed her dad and continued pacing while it rang. She'd already told him she had a new number, lying and saying that she'd accidentally smashed her phone on the street. Dante crushing it against the wall was no accident.

It took a moment to pick up and a familiar voice made her

relax a little.

"Mary." He said softly and she smiled.

"Hey, Dad."

While they chatted small talk, Mary contemplated how she'd tell her dad about Dante's return. She knew he was not Dante's biggest fan, especially after the murder attempt ten years ago, but she really needed some advice.

"So I have a problem," Mary said quietly and she heard him sitting down in the background.

"Go on."

Mary bit her lip and hesitated. She took a deep breath and said the words she'd been dreading.

"Dante's back."

There was a moment of silence and she held her breath, her dad barely ever lost his temper, but Dante was a point of contention for him.

"And when you say 'back', do you mean in Neverfield?"

"No," she sighed. "He's in the city, he just joined the firm."

"Your firm?"

"The very one."

Alan let out a slow breath and Mary fretted, she knew this wouldn't be an easy conversation.

"I assume he's been up to his usual charming antics." The sarcasm in her dad's tone caught Mary off guard, he was usually a peace-loving, kind man and this was not him. Something was off and she could smell it.

"What aren't you telling me?"

"It's nothing, I-"

He cut himself off and Mary waited patiently. She knew there was more to Dante than met the eye, she was certain he was different, she just wasn't sure how, but she guessed her dad knew more than he was letting on.

There was a pause on the end of the line before Alan spoke again.

Inferno

"Why don't you come back for the weekend?"

Sighing, Mary considered it. She hadn't been home for such a long time and although she was sure that her dad missed her, a part of her resisted going back. She'd shed her Neverfield skin and she didn't want it back.

But she couldn't stay in the city, she couldn't stand another moment with Dante in her office. She was suffocating with him, on the verge of losing her shit for real.

"Sure." She sighed, resigned to the fact that going back to Neverfield was a better option than sitting around on the weekend thinking Dante harassing her. Plus, he could easily find out where she lived and she didn't want him anywhere near her.

They hung up and Mary popped open a bottle of wine, pouring herself a generous glass before getting undressed to shower. She needed to relax, get through this week and then see her dad again and get the answers she deserved.

As she ran her hand under the water while she waited for it to heat up, Mary pondered her feelings about returning home. She was anxious to see how much had changed in her absence. Or would it be just the same, like a time capsule that had been preserved while she got on with her life? She wasn't sure.

After holding her fingers under the showerhead for ten minutes, Mary frustratedly conceded that the water wasn't warming up and dried off her icy cold fingers. *Could this day really get any worse?*

She made a note in her phone to call her landlord first thing in the morning and packed a small shower bag before calling a taxi and heading to the office.

The office was dark and quiet, but because Monica loved to hit the gym before the workday started, she'd got some showers installed so she could freshen up after her intense workouts.

Mary had a key for the main building and her boss had told her to use the showers whenever. Up until now, she'd had no reason to, but today was the day she'd been showering in the office it seemed. As if her day could reach rock bottom anymore if it tried.

Finding the floor empty, Mary made her way to the shower rooms which were joined onto the restrooms. She flicked on the bright fluorescent lights, then closed the door and began to peel off her casual clothes. As she ran the water, steam filled the room, creating a comfortable haze and Mary stepped into the cubicle, sighing as the hot water soothed her tense shoulders.

Today had been a complete mind fuck. On one hand, Mary was very tempted to report Dante for his ridiculous behavior in the apartment but then on the other, she was drawn in by his touch, curious about his past and tempted by his allure.

She shook her head fiercely, in a desperate attempt to forget his hot tongue on her ear, caressing her skin and how much she'd loved it. Mary hated herself for how her body acted around Dante, he set her alight from the inside out and she burned for him.

Thinking about how Dante's hands felt on hers, she closed her eyes and let her fingers slip down her body, tracing the contours of her shape as she caressed her skin, imagining it was Dante's hands on her. She breathed deeply, inhaling the steam as she palmed her breast, squeezing and pinching it. Mary moaned airily before dipping her hand lower and grazing her nails over her sensitive body.

Her skin felt charged with lust and need, her breaths came in short pants as she teased herself, visualizing Dante's rough hands holding her neck, his lips on her breasts, tugging roughly, his fingers wandering down her lower body, grazing

Inferno

her skin, leaving trials of fire in their wake as he caressed her most sensitive part…

A loud bang interrupted Mary from her self-pleasure and her eyes snapped open, her lust-filled haze vanishing as her heart thumped erratically in her chest at the thought of someone in there with her. She was embarrassed to be touching herself in the showers at work where anyone who had a key could walk in- Hell, Monica herself could stroll right in and hear Mary's moans. It was so inappropriate, but her body ached for release after her tension with Dante, she throbbed painfully and she blew out a frustrated breath.

Leaving the shower running, Mary leaned out of the cubicle and listened for a second. She was met with silence, the only clear sound was the water hitting the shower floor and the fan buzzing in the room.

"Hello?" She called out, feeling stupid, but anxious that someone had been watching her in the shower. Her gaze fell on the door, it was open ajar and she frowned, specifically remembering that she'd closed it. Goosebumps rippled over her skin and the hair at the back of her neck stood on end.

Someone was in there.

Mary stepped out of the shower, hastily grabbed her towel off the hook next to it, and tiptoed closer to the door. She glanced around, feeling like an idiot for being so uptight, but she was sure she'd locked that door. She pushed it shut with a click, sliding the lock in place, and sighed, pressing her forehead to the door.

Suddenly, a hand covered her mouth, panic bubbled up in her and she instinctively kicked out behind her, feeling a large body pushing her into the door. The floor was slippery underneath her bare feet, making her attempts at kicking her attacker feeble.

In a mad frenzy, she sank her teeth into their hand, tasting the salty, smokey skin and the attacker reeled their hand away. Whilst gripping her towel for dear life, Mary threw her head back in an attempt to knock them away. It caught their chin and they cursed loudly, stumbling back and away from her.

Mary froze for a moment, recognizing that voice.

No fucking way.

She spun around, enraged, and was face to face with him. Dante rubbed his chin with his hand and glared at her.

"What the fuck are you doing here?" She yelled at him and his eyebrow quirked, that was the first time he'd heard her curse, and damn if it didn't make him want to take her there and then. Hearing those words fall out of her pretty mouth was *hot*.

"I was finishing up in the office and heard the shower running, figured someone had left it on, so I came to investigate." He shrugged, his eyes wandering greedily over the vast expanse of her skin that was on show."

And then you decided to attack me from behind?"

"Actually I believe it was you who attacked me there, and ouch, by the way, that hurt."

Mary rolled her eyes and stared at him. He'd shed his leather jacket, wearing only his black shirt which was unbuttoned halfway down his broad torso, exposing a delicious amount of tanned, lean skin.

The sleeves were rolled up, showing off his tattoos which ran down the length of his forearms and disappeared under his shirt. Her curiosity peaked and she wondered whether his tattoos stopped at his arms or whether his whole torso was inked. She bit her lip, getting hot and bothered again, just thinking about him shirtless.

He was beyond delicious, devious. He was a walking sin and Mary was about to commit heresy.

There was no way he was still working here this late and

Inferno

Mary hadn't seen any of the lights on, she didn't doubt Dante was insane enough to work in the dark, but his story felt too much like a lie.

"Were you following me?"

Dante ignored her question, his eyes leisurely making their way down her towel-clad body. Mary pulled the thin material closer to herself, feeling heated and equally annoyed by Dante's eyes on her. She was confused, she hated him, hated their history but couldn't ignore the hot, painful tension between them. It was like a bow strung too tightly. She knew it would snap eventually and she needed to be far away from Dante and his hot body, so she didn't make any stupid mistakes.

She was about to make him leave so she could dress in privacy without his wandering gaze when he interrupted her.

"Who were you thinking about?"

Mary blinked, confused for a moment.

"Who were you thinking about in the shower?" He whispered, his voice low, eyes dark. "While you were touching yourself."

Mary felt the flush burn into her skin, crawling up her neck and blossoming across her cheeks. She was more than mortified that Dante had heard her. She was never, ever going to admit that it was him who'd got her flustered. That it was the thought of his hands on her body, his lips on her neck that had her aching for release.

"I bet it was me. After our little run-in earlier, I was pretty turned on too." He smirked and stepped forward towards Mary. She inched back, but her body bumped against the door, trapping her in again for the second time today. She glanced over Dante's shoulder, looking for an escape route, but came up empty-handed. The door was the only way out, and the look in Dante's eyes told her she wasn't leaving without a fight.

He prowled closer, his arms caging her in. Mary gritted her teeth, her heart beating fast in her chest. How was it that in the space of less than a day, she was pressed up against a wall, caught in Dante's games again?

With one white-knuckled hand gripping her towel, she pushed his chest away with the other, not wanting him any closer. He clouded her thoughts and her mind mind was on one track right now, this fine specimen in front of her and how he could help her find some release.

Her hand a little too long on his torso, feeling the hard ridges of his sculpted body under her fingers. His skin felt hot under her palm, and Dante's lip tugged into a smirk as he pressed his chest into her touch.

Leaning in, he pinned his body to hers and ran the tip of his nose down the length of her neck. Mary shivered, goosebumps rising on her skin as his hot breath tickled her sensitive skin and Dante breathed her in. Her scent was so alluring, being this close made his head spin with lust, desire, and something more sinister.

Closing her eyes, Mary's heart thumped in her chest, she scrunched up the front of his shirt in her hand, fisting the material in an attempt to push him away or pull him closer? At this point, she didn't know. His hands wandered down her body and gripped her waist, the thin towel did nothing to protect her skin from the searing heat of his touch.

She smelled smoke in the air, it mixed with the steam from the still running shower and she faintly remembered the day she saw him leaving the principal's office, smoke rising from his angry body. Huh, so she hadn't made that up.

His hot tongue licked the beads of water off her shoulder and she let out a deep breath, succumbing to the feeling of his body pressed against hers. It felt amazing, there was no doubt about that, his strong thighs pressed to her pelvis and he pushed his knee between her legs urging them apart. She spread wider for him as his hands wandered up her body, fingers brushing the swell of her breast.

Mary's breath hitched and Dante's eyes searched her face; her eyes were closed, lips parted and she emitted a gentle glow that made her skin look luminescent. He smirked to himself, knowing this was just the beginning.

Running his tongue down past her collarbone, Dante pulled down the towel and Mary let him, much to her surprise. It exposed her chest and stomach, resting on her hips. She automatically reached for it, feeling too exposed as her nipples beaded in the cool air, but before she could pull it back up, hot lips clamped down on her breast, causing her to let out a moan- much louder than she expected.

She felt Dante smirk against her skin and she had a snarky retort on her tongue but as his teeth grazed her nipple, the words were lost in another moan. The tendrils of her denied orgasm crept back, her body setting alight from the inside.

It had been far too long since Mary had been touched like this. Blood rushed in her ears, her body almost shook from his touch. Her skin felt too tight like her body was caging her in and she wanted to crawl out of it.

Dante let her breast go before continuing his sensual assault on the other, his hands roamed down to her lower back and hips, pulling him closer to his body and the towel slipped away, leaving Mary completely bare to him. A gasp escaped her lips as he brushed his fingers over her lower stomach, making their way down to where she wanted him the most.

He took a step back to admire this goddess in front of him, his gaze ran down her body. The room felt charged, and Mary opened her eyes to see Dante's burning expression. It was her, she made him feel like that. She felt a small amount of victory that her body could make him weak. His face almost lit up, a light casting a glow on it from underneath and she frowned, glancing down at her naked body.

Not again, she groaned as her skin glowed gently like a glow stick, even in the bright fluorescents, it was obvious. She wondered why Dante hadn't run for the hills when he'd seen her skin glowing. But that thought quickly flew away as she frustratedly bent down and grabbed the towel from the floor. The spell between them broke in a second, leaving them both wanting more.

Embarrassment flooded her as she pulled on her sweatshirt and leggings as fast as possible. They stuck to her damp, flushed skin but she didn't care. She felt Dante's eyes on her as she slipped on her clothes, desperate to get out of there. It had been a mistake to let him touch her, to let her walls down for a second.

She switched off the shower and the deafening silence between seemed to stretch on forever.

Dante watched Mary's demeanor change from needy and pliable to embarrassed and shut off. He thought about why she was embarrassed, the tension was so obvious between the two of them, why couldn't she just give in? He'd cracked down a wall inside her though, he knew it and so did she. They couldn't go back, not now he'd touched her, he'd made her feel good and more importantly, she'd *liked* it.

"When's the last time someone touched you like that Mary Mack? Made you feel good?" His tone was taunting and Mary felt even more embarrassed, she remembered exactly how long it'd been and she would *not* be giving Dante the satisfaction of an answer.

"Soon enough, you'll be begging for me."

Mary spun to face him, her wet hair hanging around her face like a veil. She stared at him through the brown and white strands as he leaned against the door, hands shoved in his pockets.

"I'll never beg for you Dante Enfter. That's something you can count on."

She picked up her bag, her eyes not leaving his and she pushed him out of the way as slid across the bathroom lock and threw open the door. Not giving him a second glance, she stormed out of the office with her head held high. She got a taxi home and packed quickly, throwing all her clothes and toiletries into a suitcase.

Mary called Monica first, announcing that something had come up so she needed to take emergency leave. She'd never taken a day off in the office, so Monica gave her the week off without question. She then called her dad, telling him she'd be arriving tonight.

Without another thought, Mary dragged her suitcase down to her car in the basement, slid into the driver's seat, and braced herself for the four-hour drive back to Neverfield with nothing but her thoughts of Dante to keep her company..

Chapter Eight: Hell

Ten Years Ago

Materializing in the dark room, Dante inhaled the smell of decay and smoke. Home.

His arrival did not go unnoticed though, and a flurry of demons crashed into the room mere seconds after. He'd decided to appear in the East wing, hoping he'd be able to lay low until he'd seen what had gone on since he'd left. It had been five years since he'd seen those black walls and smelt the stench of death that hung in the air. He'd missed it.

"Your Highness, your mother is waiting in the Grand Hall for you." A short, fat, red-skinned demon bowed and indicated for Dante to follow him.

"Did Ashja arrive with you?" It asked, looking around the Prince in case it'd missed Dante's fallen accomplice.

"Ashja is in the Outer now."

The demon blinked for a second, its four eyes working in sync before it nodded and gestured for Dante to follow. The three other demons that had arrived at the same time, murmured about Ashja and what had happened to her. Dante paid them no attention as they snaked through the palace walls. He didn't want to think about her lifeless eyes staring at him as the silver knife shone in her chest. He didn't like how it made him feel.

They arrived at the Grand Hall and the red demon, known as Zorax, opened the door for Dante and followed behind him, keeping his head low.

The Grand Hall was the staple room of the palace, the room where all important meetings, and events, such as sacrifices or beheadings were held. At the very end sat a charcoal stone throne, built upon steps made out of a heap of bones and with two skulls on either side of the headrest.

Legend had it they were angel skulls, but Dante didn't believe such a myth. He'd never met an angel, but he was sure they would have put up one hell of a fight and would very much object to having their skulls mounted onto a throne in Hell.

And upon the throne sat Persephone. Her long raven hair flowed around her body, her dark skin and sharp talons made her stand out among the demons- that was what defined the royal bloodline; their human features.

Most demons were very identifiable from their wings, talons, horns, tails, skin color, and the like. The Royals mostly resembled humans with only subtle features like their eye color- or in Persephone's case her long nails- to indicate their demonic existence.

Like his mother before him, Dante had the same eyes, but aside from his magic and powers, it was the only thing that made him different from a human. Something that was easy to disguise to help him blend in with the human world.

A group of researchers stood in front of the Queen. Dante could tell who they were by their dark red robes. The demon skills were defined by the color they wore, similarly to a hospital and different color scrubs like on Earth.

"So you're telling me that all this reading the signs, blood sacrifices, consulting the fire and you're no closer to finding the damn book?!"

Dante watched his mother slowly lose her cool. She wasn't a particularly well-tempered woman to start with, and something had really got under her skin this time.

"W-We've been doing all we can your Highness if we just had a little more time-"

"'We've been doing all we can'" She mocked. "Well, We don't have time, the prophecy is predicted soon, it could be a matter of days!" She fiercely shot up from her throne, her robes swirling around her menacingly and the researchers cowered.

"Get it sorted now." She seethed and sat back down on her throne.

She dismissed them with a wave of her hand. They nodded collectively, and shuffled out of the room, mumbling about consulting the Oracle again.

Dante stepped closer to the throne once the doors had shut and Persephone watched him, eyes as sharp as daggers. He was still shirtless, his spells inked all over his upper body. His skin was darkened by the smoke from the fire; smudges of ash and grime on his face.

"Well you better give me some good news."

Dante never expected a warm greeting from his mother after five years away, but he didn't care much for her callous tone.

"Ashja is in the Outer."

His mother pursed her dark lips and looked around the sparse hall, a bored expression painted across her face.

"Nope, that's not good news. Try again."

"I got kicked out of high school."

Inferno

"You've got one more chance Dante before I lose my temper."

"An assassin tried to kill me."

Persephone eyes sparkled, she sat upright on the throne and beckoned him closer.

Stepping forward until he was at the foot of the throne. His mother watched him like a hawk, eyes sharp and beady. He waited whilst she tapped her sharp talons against the armrest. They clicked on the stone, the sound echoing in the empty room.

"Well, tell me. What did this assassin look like?"

"He was dressed like a priest; a dog collar and a giant silver cross- you know the look."

"Did he say what he wanted?"

"He didn't talk much." Dante shrugged, not caring about the whys involved with the attempted assassination. He'd survived, the killer hadn't and that was that.

Persephone leaned back in the throne, face thoughtful. She suddenly snapped her fingers and two guards stood to attention next to her.

"Find me The Vicar."

They bowed and marched out of the room, the sound of their footsteps thudded on the stone floor. Dante watched them leave then spun back to face his mother.

"So you know him."

She smiled a hard, cruel smile that made Dante remember how unmotherly she'd been to him in the past.

"Of course, he's famous for killing our kind. Although he's no match for my boy." Cruel pride laced her words.

Persephone only cared for her son when it involved violence or victory. He was a pawn in her games, which he'd learned pretty early on in his life. Once his father had died, young Dante had sought out his mother's affection, of which he had been denied again and again. Persephone only ever wanted to see him when he became of use.

So Dante had dedicated his time to fighting, training, and learning his powers. He'd been locked up in the castle, so he'd had no friends. All the demon servants were too scared to speak to him; they didn't want to face Persephone's wrath. Bron had been his one friend, who had trained him, helped him learn and harness his powers, and had been a sympathetic ear.

But when he was sent to Earth, Dante heard that Persephone had executed Bron for making Dante weak. She'd said that he needed enemies to be strong, not friends.

Gazing at his mother now, he realized that she was not strong, she was weak. Using her powers as fear to gain allegiance. He knew his father had ruled as a fair King of Hell, well, as fair as you can be when you're ruling the underworld, and that the demons had mourned his loss deeply.

"What else did you learn in your time in that pitiful place?" Her sharp word interrupted his thoughts and Dante watched her sit back down on her throne, looking down at him with her black eyes.

"There was a girl."

With a bored expression, Persephone gazed at her nails; long sharp, black talons which Dante had seen in action and didn't want to be on the receiving end of any time soon.

He'd once witnessed his mother lose her temper on a maid and she'd slashed the demon's head right off in one clean movement. Yep, it was safe to say he didn't desire such a sticky ending for himself.

"Dante, I don't care for your pathetic human conquests, tell me something of importance."

"She glowed."

Her black eyes narrowed as Dante observed his mother's

Inferno

reaction. He knew Mary was something more than human and the way his mother's interest piqued, confirmed his suspicions.

"Tell me more."

"She had white hair, silver eyes and she glowed. That's all I know."

"Her name?"

"Mary Lux."

Sitting bolt upright, Persephone called for a guard to bring the group of researchers back.

"You'll tell me everything about her. Every little detail."

"Not until you tell me why I should."

Her eyes narrowed again at her son, he'd grown a backbone whilst away and she wasn't sure she liked it.

After a few moments of tense silence where Dante thought his mother might rip him a new one, Persephone opened her mouth.

"Fine. Come with me."

Stepping down from the throne, she stalked towards the main doors, her heels clicking against the floor and Dante fell in line behind her.

He followed her around the winding corridors of the palace, it hadn't changed much since he'd been gone. The dark walls of the castle which kept the lesser demons out and kept Dante in were still the same. He was mainly pissed off that he'd had to come back to Hell so soon, he thought he'd have another chance at killing Mary first.

After several sets of stairs, they entered a part of the castle that Dante had been forbidden to go to when he was younger; the North Wing. When he'd asked why he'd been rewarded with a slap on his cheek from his mother, so he'd stopped asking any questions pretty quickly.

They halted in front of a pair of double doors and Persephone raised her hand, the talon on her forefinger extended in length and she inserted it into a small slit in the wood, hidden to the naked eye. The door clanked and she retracted her hand, tucking it back into her robe.

The doors slowly swung open, revealing a large room with dark stone and a wooden desk in the center. The walls were littered with shelves containing different books, jars with unblinking eyes, inks, and other magical items that Dante had either never seen before or never wanted to see again.

Sitting behind the desk, his mother gestured for him to take a seat in front of her as if he were at a job interview and she was the one asking the questions.

"This, Dante, is my workroom, it's where I collect rare items, consult the Oracle, and where I learned about the prophecy."

"Prophecy?" Dante's interest piqued and he leaned in closer as his mother pulled a wooden box from under the desk. It wasn't big, but it looked important with unknown markings and intricate carvings running across the lid and sides.

"And this, my dear, is the Oracle."

Pressing a latch, the box almost fell apart, all four sides opening up to reveal a glowing glass cube within.

"Tell me the prophecy." She spoke to the box and Dante watched in wonder as the lights inside it swirled around, creating patterns. It was mesmerizing.

"With devastation and ruin, an unlikely alliance of the Hellish offspring and a daughter of God will renew the scorched Earth."

The words didn't ring a bell in Dante's mind and he stared blankly at his mother, wondering if she was messing around with him. Although Persephone was not one to joke, she also wasn't exactly kind either and she reveled in humiliating people.

She leaned back in her chair, studying Dante's expression as she clasped her hands together.

"You see, I want to take Earth and destroy mankind; that useless species. But this prophecy seems to say that my plans of making Earth mine won't go particularly well if a daughter of God and a Hellish offspring align. I need to stop that."

Dante's thoughts flew to Mary, although he didn't know much about the angels, he knew she had something to do with them. Could the prophecy be about her?

An evil smile spread over his lips as he thought about killing her but for real this time and not only appeasing his mother in the process but also stopping a stupid, age-old prophecy from coming to fruition.

"Now this girl, this Mary Lux. I want you to tell me everything you know about her."

Chapter Nine: Fight

Ten Years Ago

The news of the fire spread through the high school like a raging river. The police had said they'd found a body, but it was hard to identify, so nothing was confirmed. Everyone speculated, but no one really knew the truth.

Mary listened to the idle gossip in the cafeteria, Ally talking to and sympathizing with half of the female population of Neverfield High. They swooned about Dante, some even cried.

But Mary couldn't shake the feeling that he wasn't dead.

The threat that had hung in the air when he'd left the principal's office yesterday was still spinning around her head like a broken record. She didn't really know Dante, but she knew he wouldn't die in a simple house fire, it was too… mundane?

Class whizzed by and Mary found herself not taking the bus home, but instead going up the hill, to the charred remains of Dante's house. Something inside her told her that she needed to see it for herself, not that his body would be there for her

Inferno

to inspect, but she just had to see something.

The bus dropped her off near the entrance and the wrought iron gates creaked as she pushed them open. The fire crew had put out the blazing inferno but it still smoked, tainting the Spring blue sky with its grey plumes. The skeleton of the house, with its burnt timbers and glowing embers, it still looked as menacing as it had when it was built.

Mary and Ally had once believed the house to be haunted when they were in fifth grade. They'd made a pact on Halloween to do a paranormal investigation, but as soon as they'd trudged up the hill, breathless and sweaty in their Halloween costumes, they'd been spooked by the wind blowing the gate open and they'd bolted like they'd seen a real ghost.

Since then, they'd avoided it and it'd remained empty until Dante moved in four years ago. His sudden arrival caused a commotion in the town- speculation about who he was; a nobody, the boy with no parents. Mary had pitied him at first, but then his torment on her had begun and she'd soon felt nothing but contempt for him.

"Excuse me, you can't be here, this is an active crime scene." An officer, not far off Mary's age, walked towards her. He'd probably been put on patrol; basically the worst job.

"I'm just leaving." She stared at the house one more time, feeling an electrical buzz in the air. She smelled the smoke, yes, but something else too. Something tangier, but she couldn't put her finger on it.

Hoisting her bag onto her shoulder, Mary turned as the wind blew something at her feet. She bent down, picking up a large blue feather.

Inspecting it, she twisted it in her fingers, holding it by the stem, trying to place which bird it had come from. They didn't have any exotic animals in Neverfield and Mary knew some people kept pets like parrots, but the feather was far too

Violet E.C

big for a parrot. It was at least the side of her forearm, large and soft. As she reached out to stroke the feathers, an electric shock stung her fingers. It didn't hurt but wasn't pleasant either. She quickly retracted her hand back, frowning at the tingles that lingered.

Gently tucking the feather into her bag, making sure not to touch it again, Mary made her way back to the bus stop.

∽

Lounging on Mary's bed, Ally was reading the latest issue of some paranormal magazine that she'd pinched from the store her parents owned. She lay on her stomach, flicking through the pages as she glanced at the pictures that swore they'd caught a ghost on camera.

"Oh would you listen to this, someone wrote in saying that they think their boyfriend is a demon in disguise. Like, come on, who actually believes this stuff? Why do they even publish it?"

Mary stared absentmindedly out the window, twisting the stem of the feather in her fingers. She was deep in thought, wondering why her mind kept going back to the smoldering house. She could see the smoke from her window, still floating in the air although the house was hidden by the trees around it.

"Earth to Mary." Ally waved her magazine in front of Mary's face and she turned to look at her friend.

"Sorry, I was thinking."

"A dangerous thing to do." Ally giggled and Mary smiled softly, twisting her chair around so she was looking back at Ally. She sat with her legs crossed, chewing a Twizzler as she watched her best friend. Mary was zoned out, her mind elsewhere and Ally didn't like that.

Inferno

"So, did you apply to NCC?"

NCC was Neverfield's Community College and most people who planned on staying in Neverfield for the rest of their lives went there, studied some useless program, got married straight after, and lived in the drab town forever.

Mary sighed, she'd talked her dad into letting her apply for other colleges outside the town. He wanted her in the same state, but she didn't have to be in the town itself. So she'd applied to every single college that wasn't in Neverfield.

She hadn't told Ally though, she knew her best friend would be gutted if she told her she was leaving, so she'd kept it a secret. But graduation and finals were fast approaching and Mary knew she couldn't hide her plans forever.

"No…" She said tentatively and Ally's head popped up from the magazine, she studied Mary for a moment. She knew Mary didn't like it there, but she'd been hoping she'd change her mind.

"'No' isn't the right answer, try again."

"Ally-"

"Is Neverfield that bad for you, Maz?"

Ally sat up and stared at her best friend, she felt the sting of betrayal in her heart as she realized that they wouldn't be going to college together. Ally and Mary had been best friends through thick and thin, she needed her best friend by her side, but it seemed like Mary had other plans.

"What do I have here Ally? My dad would rather spend his time with his books, he doesn't need a daily living reminder of his dead wife. Dante tried to drown me last week, everyone at school thinks I'm a freak, I don't fit in here. I never have."

"And what about me? You have me."

"And you have Mark, you don't need me."

Mary looked out of the window again, dreaming she was somewhere else, somewhere she belonged.

Violet E.C

"But what about my best friend? You don't think I need her?" Ally's voice cracked, she looked wounded and Mary tried to reconcile.

"Of course, but you have your family, the store-"

"So that's it then? You're just gonna leave?"

"You could come with me," Mary suggested, hopeful. She didn't want to stay, but it didn't mean Ally had to either.

"I can't, I have my family here, plus Mark."

"Exactly."

It was a pointless conversation. Mary couldn't stay and Ally couldn't leave.

In Mary's head, she had always known Ally would stay here. Her future was predetermined; She'd stay in Neverfield, go to college there, get married there, have her kids there, and die there. That was what people did in a small town and that was exactly what Mary couldn't stand.

"What bird do you think this feather came from?" A change of conversation was what they needed to relieve the tension in the room.

"Who cares about some feather? You're leaving me." Ally sulked, opening up the magazine again and Mary sighed, tired of fighting.

"Well if you're ignoring me, then I'll just have to go toast some Pop-Tarts by myself."

Her best friend's head snapped up from behind her magazine. Mary grinned, knowing Ally couldn't resist a good Pop-Tart. Her best friend reluctantly untangled herself from the blanket and tried to resist a smile.

And just like that, their friendship was right again, for now.

∽

Pushing open the school front doors, Mary sighed happily.

Inferno

The sun was shining, the sky was bright blue and school was over. Finally.

Her finals had gone by in a flash of studying, stress, and lots of Pop-Tarts. She and Ally had spent some evenings studying together, although Ally always whined that she wanted to go and see Mark. Mary couldn't force her to study, but she always added on the offer of Pop-Tarts to sweeten the deal in a desperate attempt to help her best friend pass school. She felt it was the best she could do, considering she was leaving at the end of summer whether Ally liked it or not.

They'd been avoiding the topic of college and Mary's plans to leave for weeks. Every time someone asked Mary about college, Ally would leave or turn away, not wanting to hear that her best friend was ditching her in a few months.

She wasn't only upset about that, she was jealous that Mary had a bright future ahead of her when Ally knew she'd probably inherit her parent's store and work there for the rest of her life. Her future seemed bleak compared to Mary's and she didn't like that.

Hands clamped down on her shoulders and Ally jumped in front of Mary, grinning like the Cheshire Cat.

For a second, Mary's heartbeat picked up and she panicked, thinking about Dante drowning her. She thought she'd got through it, but at night the dreams were vivid, her near-death experience haunting her.

That and the thought that Dante wasn't dead made her glance at the shadow out of the corner of her eye or double-check the locks were bolted on the doors and windows. Yep, she'd got a bit paranoid, but who could blame her?

"So, how are we celebrating finishing finals?" Ally brushed her bangs out of her face, she grinned a mischievous smile.

"What do you have planned, Ally?"

"Oh, nothing big." She grinned. "Just a party at Jesse's."

Jesse's house.

Mary's mind flew back to the last time she'd been there, four months ago. How Dante had tried to drown her in the pool.

The school and town had moved on from Dante's death, but she was still bothered by it. She just knew he wasn't dead, but she didn't know how to explain it. His presence still followed her, lurking in the shadows, out of reach but never gone.

Aside from that, her last few months at school had been blissful though, Dante's minions had backed off since their leader was gone and she'd had a bullying-free experience which had been so very peaceful.

She hesitated though, not sure about going back to Jesse's house after everything.

"I don't know-"

"Come on, Dante's dead and you need to live a little, we just finished school!" Ally's pining for Dante had dried up pretty quickly as had every other girl's sadness once the town moved on. They'd even held a stupid vigil for him. Mary had pictured Dante laughing in Hell at the townspeople singing and holding candles in their hands. She hadn't attended.

Ally grinned, waving her hands dramatically while she tried to convince her that the party was a good idea.

"… and plus this could be the last time we party together."

And there it was. The guilt-tripping statement, paired with the puppy dog eyes that made Mary concede defeat.

"Okay."

Squealing, Ally jumped up and down on the spot as they walked towards the bus and began to plan what they'd wear.

The party was in full swing by the time Ally, Mary and Mark

Inferno

showed up. Drunk kids stumbled around Jesse's house, sloshing their drinks everywhere and making out with whoever they could find- it was kind of gross.

Making a beeline for the drinks table, Mary poured them all mixers. She'd been sucked into Ally's fashion mission so she was wearing an outfit she'd never normally had picked; blue flared jeans and a white cami top which revealed way too much for Mary's liking, so she'd brought a cardigan along, pulling it around her shoulders and hiding her most of her skin, much to Ally's chagrin.

Mary hated that so much of her skin could be on show in the dark, where it would glow and be insanely obvious. She needed to keep it on the down-low.

The thumping beat was already giving Mary a headache, she hadn't been to Jesse's parties since the last incident. Everyone said he threw the best, but she soon realized that was because he invited anyone and everyone.

"Here's to no more school!" Ally yelled and they all lifted their plastic cups in the air before chugging the cheap alcohol that burned down their throats.

Ally and Mark branched off, holding each other close on the dancefloor and Mary wandered around, avoiding feeling like a third wheel. Seeing familiar faces, she smiled at some, danced with a couple of others, but found herself walking out the back doors, towards the pool.

The water glittered in the fading sun, the pool illuminated by pale lights under the surface. Mary stared at her reflection, vividly remembering the panic, the burn in her lungs, the weight on her shoulders. She almost felt a phantom hand holding her neck, gently squeezing and she shook her head.

"It's kind of peaceful, isn't it?"

Mary jumped back from the water's edge, a guy she hadn't seen before was standing beside her, gazing at the water. She didn't want to stare, but he was undoubtedly handsome. His hair was the same color as hers, which surprised her. It was gelled back, showing off his amazing bone structure; high cheekbones, a strong nose, and a jawline that could cut glass. He was beautiful, there really was no other way to describe it and her heart thudded in her chest unexpectedly, like it knew him.

She was quiet for a moment, contemplating her thoughts. She didn't want to embarrass herself in front of this fine specimen.

"Do you go to the high school?"

The boy faltered for a second, and a flash of confusion spread across his features before his face was a mask again; cool and calm. Mary studied him closely, her heart still thumping in her chest.

"Kind of."

Okay, not the answer Mary was expecting, but she decided not to push it. Maybe he was being evasive for a reason. It didn't matter anyway, she was here to have fun.

"I'm Mary." She stuck out her hand, smiling as she gazed at him.

"I'm Turiel."

His hand met hers and a familiar feeling came over her making her heartbeat slow, her skin glowed slightly under the moonlight and she gasped as she looked into his eyes.

They were exactly the same as hers.

Jesse watched the two by the pool from his living room, seeing them shake hands and Mary's skin glow. He knew what she was, he'd known from the start. He'd let Dante antagonize her because it was fun watching the enemy squirm after all.

Dante didn't know though, he'd lived too much of a comfortable life in the palace walls to know the tell-tale signs of the Angels and especially the Nephilim.

Jesse murmured a few words, incomprehensible to the human ear and dark smoke appeared in the fireplace. Persephone's face materialized in the smoke and Jesse bowed.

"Jessamus, what do you have for me?"

"The Holies have made contact, Your Highness. One of them is here tonight."

Persephone frowned, grinding her teeth together as she tapped her nails on her desk. The smoke shifted around the image of her in his fireplace and Jesse found it hard to gauge her reaction.

"I could take it out," Jesse continued, "lure it to somewhere quiet and kill-"

"Enough. We don't want to alert them of your presence and they'll miss one of their precious angels if you go and kill it." She snapped and he ground his teeth to keep quiet. He ached to shed his skin and sink his teeth into one of the Holies.

"Keep an eye on both of them for now and tell me if any more appear." She ordered, giving him no time to reply. The smoke dissipated and Jesse sighed deeply, itching to kill the angel boy in his yard.

"As you wish, Your Highness." He grumbled as his hands curled into fists by his side.

A yell interrupted his thoughts and he glanced out of the window again. The angel was still standing next to the girl, but a human girl with dark hair was in front of her, shouting and pushing her with a finger. The girl glowed, her white hair almost luminescent as she tried to keep a lid on her powers.

Jesse closed his eyes and listened closely.

"You're just running away, always running Mary. Always have and always will." Ally slurred but her drunk words hit hard. Mary felt a strange tingle of energy coursing through her, begging to be released. Turiel put his hand on her arm, instantly grounding her. Her skin glowed brightly for a second, not noticeable for anyone who wasn't looking for it. Her glow dulled down with Turiel's contact and it felt like her powers were being gently soothed.

Violet E.C

"Calm down, she doesn't mean anything by it." His voice was soothing, like honey and it dripped down her conscience, defusing her anger.

Mary knew Ally didn't, that she was upset, hurt, and drunk, and her words were empty bullets; shells with no weight to them. But they still stung nonetheless.

Ally yelled drunk words, her sentences sloppy as she tried every insult to get a rise out of Mary, to get her to say something, do something instead of being infuriatingly passive as she always was.

"There's a reason why your mom left, I bet she couldn't stand you."

As soon as the words tumbled out of her mouth, Ally regretted it. She clamped her mouth shut, slapping her hand over it as if to try and keep the angry words from flowing out like a raging river.

Mary blinked and reeled back like she'd been smacked in the face. Ally's eyes grew wide and she started to mumble a sad excuse for an apology, tears pooling in her eyes.

Mary just shook her head and turned away. Her best friend, the one person who'd never said a bad word against her, always defended her, delivered the fatal blow. Her words cut too deep and no matter how many times she apologized, Mary wouldn't be able to accept it.

Spinning on her heel and yanking her arm away from Turiel, Mary stormed out of the yard, back into the house, and straight out into the street through the front door.

She didn't stop when both Turiel and Ally yelled for her to come back.

She didn't stop when her chest heaved and her eyes stung from the unshed tears.

She just ran into the night as her hot tears blurred her vision and the stab of betrayal made her heart ache.

Chapter Ten: Hounds of Hell

Present Day

Pulling up at the house, Mary braced herself and took a deep breath. The porch light was on, and even though it was two in the morning, she was sure her dad was anxiously awaiting her arrival.

She stepped out of the car, stretching out her cramped up legs and breathing in the familiar air of Neverfield. She hadn't been back in a decade after leaving for college in the city. She and her dad had spent the annual holidays in her condo or away, but never back here.

The front door clicked open and Alan tentatively took a step out. He wasn't sure how to gauge Mary's sudden arrival, he knew she suspected he was hiding something and he wasn't sure if she'd be mad or not. Her hurried explanation that she'd be driving back tonight was unexpected and he guessed Dante's sudden appearance back in her life had something to do with it.

Mary sleepily climbed the steps and wrapped her arms

around her dad, tired from the drive and from Dante's crazy actions this week. She sighed and Alan hugged her back, glad to have his daughter home again, if only for a moment.

After being offered copious amounts of coffee, Mary said she'd be crashing in her room and they'd talk about everything tomorrow morning. Her dad looked tired, his hair greying and he pushed his glasses up his nose with one finger. She kissed him goodnight, promising him that she wasn't hungry or thirsty before he turned out the lights and made his way to bed.

Lugging her heavy bag up the stairs, Mary saw nothing had changed in the house. It was like living in a time capsule- everything left exactly how it was ten years ago, down to the photos in the frames and the shoes in the hallway. She hurried past all the photos of herself as a kid and her bag landed on the floor with a soft thud as she reached the top of the stairs.

She pushed open the door of her bedroom, flicked on the light, and sighed. The room was as she left it; comforter folded back, dying cactus on the window sill, pictures and notes stuck on various walls, a holy cross nailed to the wall above her bed. Everything was the same.

Except it wasn't.

Dante was back and he was out for revenge it seemed. Mary's head throbbed at the thought of what had nearly happened mere hours earlier and she kicked off her shoes before flopping onto her bed without changing her clothes and falling into a deep sleep.

The next morning she woke early. The light from her undrawn blinds made her squint and she sat up before realizing she'd slept in her sweatshirt and leggings. Groaning, she checked the clock before heading for the shower. Her dad would be up soon and they'd have that all-important talk.

But first, shower then coffee.

Inferno

Dressed in some comfy pants and a t-shirt with her hair tied up in a messy bun, Mary opened the kitchen door and was transported back to the past. Her dad had laid out coffee, waffles complete with fruit, maple syrup, and juice like he did when she was stressed from school or upset. Her dad hadn't always been a model father, but he knew when things weren't right and as he always said 'there's nothing waffles can't fix'.

Grinning, she sat down at the table, gulping down the hot coffee and digging into her waffles as her dad listened to the TV in the background.

They ate in companionable silence, just as they always had. But in a way, Mary knew this was just the calm before the storm, she needed answers and her dad had been holding them from her for her whole life.

She swallowed a mouthful of food and washed it down with her coffee before clearing her throat.

"So."

Her dad looked up from his coffee mug and caught her eyes. He set it down and nodded.

"Tell me everything about this week, what Dante has said, done, anything and everything." He said.

Mary launched into her story, explaining Dante's first arrival, his threats, his actions. Of course, she left out the parts where he'd touched her, where his touch had burned her skin from the inside and made her question everything about herself.

He sipped his coffee silently while she spoke, only getting up to refill each of their mugs with more steaming coffee. Alan watched his daughter unravel, her actions more erratic as she explained how he'd smashed her phone in at the viewing. He could see Dante had got under her skin.

It was time to tell her the truth.

Alan put his mug down and sighed. Mary watched him

from across the table, her mind reeling from explaining the headache that is Dante Enfer.

"There are things" He took off his glasses, rubbing his face with both his palms. "Things beyond our comprehension."

"Okay…" Mary was wary of what her dad was talking about. She remembered his curiosity in a book when she was younger, how he'd asked every single pastor in the neighboring parishes about it. He had been obsessed and she worried that he was consumed by it after her mom had died.

"It's hard to explain, but with Dante's reappearance in your life, I'm sure worse things will follow."

"What things?" Mary was insanely frustrated. No one ever gave her a straight answer and it was driving her nuts. "Dad, you're not making any sense."

"You need to stay away from him."

Mary rolled her eyes, laughing to herself.

"Trust me, I'm trying."

There was no hint of humor in Alan's face, his mouth turned down into a frown and his eyes sharp.

"I'm serious, Mary, he's bad news."

Like she didn't already know. He'd tried to drown her for God's sake. Her dad was stating the obvious and being vague at the same time and it was so fucking annoying.

"Okay, but what about the other stuff? The book you were so interested in? What about that?"

Her dad blinked, surprised she remembered his inquiries about the book ten years ago. But Mary was observant and she didn't forget, just as he hadn't either. He hesitated, clearing his throat.

Just as he opened his mouth to speak, the doorbell rang. Mary froze, dread spiked in her and she was sure Dante had followed her and was here.

As if he'd use the doorbell and be that polite, if he wanted

Inferno

to follow her, he'd barge in or worse, sneak into her room or something.

A weird fizzle erupted in her stomach at the thought of Dante in her room, in her *bed*... She shook her head, furious with her spicy thoughts.

"Ah, yes I told Allison you were back for a little while."

"You told Ally? Dad, you know how it was between us."

"I know, but she wanted to see you anyway. Perhaps you can put it behind you two." He put his hands up in surrender and Mary sighed, knowing she'd have to face Ally someday. She wasn't sure if she was ready to forgive just yet, but ten years was long enough to ignore her best friend. Hell, she wasn't even sure she could call Ally that after all this time.

She put their conversation to the back of her mind, but she wasn't letting it go. Her dad was hiding something and she was going to get to the bottom of it, whether he liked it or not.

After that night at the party, Mary and Ally had avoided each other until Mary left. Ally was ashamed of what she'd said, angry that Mary was leaving and hurt that her best friend was moving on with her life. Mary had been angry and hurt too, but after a while, she'd just compartmentalized the emotions and got on with her packing, her planning and moved out to the city without so much as a goodbye.

Opening the front door, Mary ran her eyes over at her best friend. She was the same but different. Her eyes were ringed in dark circles, her skin was sallow and dull and her baggy clothes looked crumpled like she'd slept in them. Her unwashed hair was piled on her head in a messy bun and Ally looked like she was in dire need of a coffee.

"Maz?"

Ally, in turn, inspected Mary. Her bright white hair was a light shade of brown, her eyes still silver- Mary had for-

Violet E.C

gotten to put contacts in that morning. She was leaner like she worked out and her skin had a healthy glow even if she looked stressed out and tired.

They stared at each other for a moment, analyzing what ten years had done to one another. Suddenly Ally flung her arms around Mary's shoulders and pulled her close, crushing her. Mary laughed, embracing her best friend's familiar body.

"I'm sorry." She murmured into Mary's t-shirt and Mary nodded, she was tired of holding a grudge and ignoring her. She'd been selfish for too long, Ally's words had hurt but ten years was enough time for them not to make her heart ache anymore. She was an adult and she needed to stop holding onto the past.

Ally smelt like old cigarettes, and unwashed clothes. Mary was slightly concerned about why Ally looked so rough, she pulled her inside the house and closed the door behind them.

"I'm going to the church, I'll see you two later, are you staying for dinner, Allison?"

"Yes sir, if that's okay with you." Ally glanced over at Mary anxiously and the latter smiled, glad to have the support of her best friend back.

They said goodbye to Alan, grabbed some Pop-Tarts from the shelf, shoved them into the toaster like they were eighteen again, and carried the steaming plate up to Mary's room. Ally took her place on the crumpled bed sheets and Mary sat by the window. It was like nothing had changed.

Mary asked Ally about her life, politely listening to how much she'd predicted for Ally came true. She'd gone to Neverfield Community College to study business, graduated, worked in her parents' shop and she was still dating Mark. Again, some things really never change.

"So, tell me all." Ally squealed, excited to see her best friend after all this time. She'd regretted those words every day for

Inferno

the last ten years but she'd never been brave enough to reach out and make amends. She'd decided that Mary would be better off without her and her nasty tongue.

Mary caught her up with all her life and what had been going on. She told her about Dante's reappearance in her life, excluding yesterday's shower incident. She didn't know what to make of that yet so she put it into a different part of her brain, one that didn't demand immediate attention.

Ally sat thoughtfully, thinking about why Dante would just turn up again after all this time. She knew he had been obsessed with Mary, but after ten years and faking his death? It seemed weird and she remembered something she'd heard Mark mention when they were high one time.

"Mark told me about something Jesse said to him." She was picking her nails as she stared at her hands, avoiding Mary's gaze. She loved her best friend but her silver eyes gave her gaze an intensity that made Ally squirm. "Something about a prophecy…"

Mary looked dubiously at Ally.

"A prophecy? What are we in, medieval times? Come on, Al." Mary scoffed and turned away from Ally's ridiculous theories. She'd always bought into paranormal stuff like demons and spirits even if she acted like a skeptic sometimes.

"No seriously, he told me it included a girl with white hair."

Mary looked away from the window and watched her best friend. Her hands were twitchy, her eyes wide and her pupils dilated.

"Are you high right now?"

Ally blinked but said nothing, looking around the room, avoiding eye contact, she fidgeted with the bedsheets, scrunching them up in her hands.

"Seriously Ally? You come here to apologize and make amends and you're drugged up?"

Violet E.C

"It was just a little bit, to get me through the day-"

Mary sighed, running a hand over her face. She'd been hoping things would be the same, but they weren't. Things hadn't just changed, they'd got worse. Ally was still on drugs and by the looks of it, not just a little high ever so often.

"Are you living with Mark then, getting high and wasting your life? What about your family? Do you care about anyone but yourself?" Mary was furious that Ally had come to see her, pretended everything was okay when she was hooked on drugs, high as hell and babbling about prophecies.

"Oh, you're one to talk. You left and never came back, not for your dad, not for me. Not for anyone!"

Ally jumped off the bed, face like thunder, and glared at Mary.

"You're the most fucking selfish person I know." She spat.

And with that she slammed the door, storming out of the house and stomping down the road.

Mary sighed and flopped back in her chair. That had not gone to plan. She was mad at herself for criticizing Ally when she knew she was right, Mary had ditched everyone and never came back.

It hurt to admit it, but Ally was right and Mary had fucked it up *again*.

∽

Pushing open the thick, wooden door, Alan sat down behind his desk in the church and took a deep breath. The desk was littered with books, old and new, some passages circled in pencil with little sticky tabs poking out of the pages.

Every day Alan came here and worked tirelessly through every single text, searching for clues, for anything that could lead him to the location of the Book of Aeternum. It had been years and he'd heard nothing, but he remained hopeful.

Inferno

It was all he had left; hope.

He pinched the bridge of his nose and thought about the recent events.

Dante was back.

That in itself was pretty bad, but then he'd not only turned up again after being supposedly dead for the last ten years but had also hunted down Mary and was on a mission to make her life a living Hell. Alan knew Dante wasn't human, he knew he was a demon, he just didn't know who or what he was yet.

He'd sent the Vicar to deal with it and then he'd disappeared off the face of the Earth, presumed dead. So Dante was strong, much stronger than your average demon. That much Alan knew.

He also knew he had to tell Mary sooner or later, he'd kept her in the dark for too long. She deserved to know the truth about her mother, her heritage, her future.

Gently moving one of the books off the table, Alan picked up where he left off, reading about the first discovery of demons and the Templar knights who fought them. The text was small and hand-written by one of the knights.

He'd found the journal with the note, along with other Templar journals in the church basement, at the back of the archives, hidden in a hole in the wall which had been bricked up. Some were too old, too weathered to be legible. He'd hoped those ones contained Templar babble rather than anything of value.

Alan softly turned a yellowing page with his forefinger and thumb as a small piece of crisp paper fluttered out. It was white, showing that it was new, definitely not as old as the journals and there was spidery handwriting was scribbled across it, as if in a hurry. Alan's heart thumped as he recognized the writing. It was Eve's hand, his late wife.

The words were small and Alan scrambled under his papers and booked to find a magnifying glass. His hand grasped the wooded handle and he peered through it.

Where the hounds of Hell dare not enter, under His watchful eye in the center, you'll find what you seek.

Alan leaned back in his chair, scratching his stubbly chin. He frowned and re-read the scrap several times. Eve wasn't one for riddles and games, but he knew that she'd been followed in her last few days. She'd perhaps kept notes only she could understand. *How very helpful for her, not so much for everyone else.* He thought to himself as he stared at his wife's handwriting and traced his finger over it.

Frustrated, Alan snapped the book in his lap shut and leaped up, pacing the floor of his small room. He muttered the words over and over until he'd memorized them. *Hounds of Hell. His watchful eye. What you seek.*

Demons. Alan suddenly thought. They were often referred to as Hell Hounds in the Templar books, as demons could come in any shape or size. Flustered, he reached for the journal and stumbled over another pile of books by his desk. They tumbled to the floor and he reminded himself to tidy them up later. Alan quickly thumbed through the pages, searching for a particular passage. He ran his finger down the page and let out a "whoop" of joy as he found it.

The hounds of Hell are back. They're looking for the angels, but are destroying every one of my brethren for amusement. I don't know how long our camp will last.

They come in the dead of night, their footsteps sometimes accompanied by the sound of hooves, sometimes claws. They come in many shapes and forms, sometimes like our own and sometimes heinous abominations.

They have no fear and we are alone.

The angels won't save us.

Inferno

No one can.

It was one of the last entries from the journals and a shiver ran down Alan's spine as he imagined hordes of demons killing these Templar knights in ways unimaginable.

Somewhere demons couldn't enter, he tapped his head and looked out of the small window. The churchyard was bathed in the morning sunlight, casting ominous shadows over graves. Sculptures of gargoyles and cherubs looked over the graves, the latter looking fondly and the former scaring the dead into staying asleep.

Staring only for a moment, Alan suddenly jumped away from the window and bolted through the door to his office. The church was empty as it often was on a Tuesday morning. He raced to the altar, the sound of his brogues slapping against the stone flooring of the church echoed in the empty space.

Practically skidding to a stop, Alan drew the cross over his chest with his hand and stepped up into the pulpit. The sunlight shone through the stained glass window, making the image of the crucifixion of Christ even brighter, blazing down on the altar.

Under His watchful eye in the center.

The altar was the center of the church.

He bent down, hands searching and he pulled back the rug that covered the uneven stones that made up the floor. One stone rocked unevenly as he knelt down, searching. Pressing down with his palm, the stone's edge lifted on the opposite side like a see-saw and Alan prized it up.

Once he'd heaved the heavy slab of stone to the side, he saw a wooden box hidden under it, no more than two feet big.

Holding his breath, heart racing in his chest, Alan gently lifted the box and saw a note tucked in one of the gaps between the slats of wood.

Violet E.C

Unfolding the note, Alan read Eve's spidery writing again.
You found it, my love. Keep it safe. Like our daughter, it's very special. All my love, Eve.

Alan held his breath for at least ten seconds before letting out a deep sigh.

He'd found it.

Unclasping the lock on the box, he opened the lid to reveal cloth. He lifted the book wrapped in cloth and pulled away the protective layer. Beneath it was an ornately covered book, with golden binding and an illustration of hands clasped together on the front.

The Book of Aeternum.

Alan was almost too shocked to jump with joy, after twenty-five years of searching, he'd found the book. He'd searched every church in the state, read every book in every library. It hadn't been an easy search for the holy book, but he'd never given up. Alan could finally research the prophecy, he could learn more about Mary's gifts. He could have all the answers he'd been searching for.

He peeked inside the front cover, the book wasn't written in English but Alan had studied enough about religion and ancient languages to piece together the first page. It spoke of an Oracle which was where the prophecy had originated from. It said the Oracle had been accessible to all in the days of ancient Greece but then it had been stolen. The book didn't say who had stolen it, only that they'd use the Oracle for power rather than guidance and wisdom.

Alan closed the front page, already feeling more knowledgeable. He decided to take the book home, so he and Mary could read it together, discover her gifts and powers together. She was more likely to believe him if he had evidence.

Hastily putting the book back into the cloth and slipping it into the box, he clutched it to his chest as he made his

Inferno

way out of the church, through the heavy wooden door, and through the graveyard. His car was parked just outside the gate. Alan looked left then right, then left again to make sure no one was around. He took a deep breath and stepped through the gate, into unblessed land.

As soon as he stepped out, he knew he should go back. He had a feeling, a cold shroud came over his shoulders, a shiver ran down his spine and the hair on the back of his neck prickled. He instantly knew he'd made a mistake by taking the book from the safety of the church.

He could go back and put the book back in the church then call Mary, tell her to come by and they could read it together. Alan chastened himself for being so reckless in trying to take it away from the holy ground.

With his mind set, he turned around but faltered as dark smoke appeared around him, blocking his entrance to the church and two demons materialized out of it.

His heart thumped in his chest and he clutched the book so tightly, his knuckles were white. Alan had never seen a demon in real life before and back then, he'd counted himself lucky.

"Give us the book and we'll promise you a quick death." One hissed, its head shaped like a snake with dark green scales, sickly yellow eyes, and a forked tongue which flicked out from its razor-sharp teeth.

"But we don't always keep our promises, do we Jessamus?" The other, with dark red skin and matching red eyes, gnarled horns twisted out of his forehead and his long tail slithered around Alan's legs, tying his ankles together. His eyes roamed over the pastor hungrily.

Alan swallowed thickly, clutching the book to his chest like a life force. He wouldn't let them get the book and if he had to die trying to keep it safe, then so be it.

The first demon- Jessamus- lurched forward, swiping the

Violet E.C

box from Alan's hands. He screamed an ungodly sound as his fingers sizzled and smoked when they came in contact with the wooden box it was encased in. His tail loosened around Alan's legs as he jumped away, howling in pain.

Alan barely had time to think as the other demon, who obviously lacked half a brain and didn't notice his friend writhing in pain, clutching his smoking fingers, reached for the box too. Alan let him touch it, smelling the stench of sulfur and decay on the demon's skin. As soon as his hand came into contact with the wood, he recoiled so quickly it made Alan's vision blur. An unearthly screech ripped from his throat, and he looked down at his smoking hands, they were sizzling like cold meat in a hot pan. His tail loosened around Alan's legs as he jumped away, howling in pain.

The air stank of burned flesh and sulfur as Alan made a split decision; he flung the box across the gate and into the churchyard, it landed with a thump but remained intact. Relieved, he turned to see the two demons staggering to their feet, clutching their charred fingers, faces etched in anger.

Jessamus hissed, opening his mouth to reveal multiple rows of razor-sharp fangs as he bared his teeth at Alan.

"Smart move, Father, shame it can't save you too."

Without thinking about it, Alan ran for his car, darting around the demons in an attempt to save himself, but they were too fast, the red one grabbing his ankles with his tail and sweeping Alan up so he was dangling upside down. His glasses slipped off his nose and they cracked as Jessamus stamped on them with his hooved feet, crunching them into the gravel.

The blood rushed to Alan's head, thundering in his ears and his silver crucifix slipped out of his shirt, dangling in front of his face, hanging from the chain around his neck. The demons flinched at the sight of it, before flinging him across the road and into a large oak tree. Alan's body cracked and sagged

Inferno

to the ground like a rag doll. He didn't move.

The demons glanced again at the book in the churchyard. Jessamus took a tentative step over the gate but recoiled back like lightning when his hoof set on instant fire. He snarled angrily and put his palms together, disappearing in the black smoke. The red demon glanced around and followed in suit. The book lay in the churchyard, safe for now.

~

Mary glanced at the clock on the wall; 6 pm. Her dad said he'd be home for dinner and it was getting late. She'd been in a bad mood all afternoon, sulking around the house after her argument with Ally. She was mainly mad at herself, Ally had been right and Mary didn't like to hear it. Her mood had only worsened when her dad hadn't returned on time.

She knew he got lost in his books in the church and tended to forget about time and that annoyed her further, just adding to her foul mood.

She ran her hand through her hair, frustrated and she went to get her phone. Checking her messages, she called her dad again but it went straight to voicemail.

Slamming her phone down, Mary wondered whether coming back to Neverfield was a good idea. She didn't have any friends here and her one best friend was mad at her again. She sighed, maybe she should have just stayed away.

Her ringtone interrupted her thoughts. A number she didn't recognize was calling her and she answered it tentatively.

"Hello?"

"Mary, it's Ally. You've got to come quickly to the hospital. It's your dad."

Chapter Eleven: Earth, Heaven and Hell

Present Day

The hospital stank of sanitizer and death, Mary struggled to breathe through her mouth as she wound through the never-ending corridors to find her dad.

She all but threw open the door to his room, sobbing when she saw him lying there, bandaged up and connected to so many different machines, the wires crawling all over him like vines, trapping him to the bed.

Seeing his daughter so upset, Alan gently shifted his head to the side, wincing in pain. Mary grasped his hand softly, eyes glassy as she looked on the verge of a breakdown. She couldn't lose another parent, not now when everything was turning upside down.

"Hey, Dad." She whispered and he smiled slightly, licking his cracked lips.

"You need to fetch the book-" His voice was hoarse, his mouth dry and his mind foggy.

Inferno

"What book, Dad?" Mary leaned closer.

"The book, in the churchyard, take it to Pastor Nolan. His number is in my office, he'll keep it safe."

Mary nodded, patting her dad's hand. She suspected he was a little out of it with all the painkillers he'd been given and was probably babbling, but she decided to go home first, then walk to the church and see if there was some random book lying around.

Reluctantly Mary left him in good hands, she knew there was nothing else she could do for him so she went home for the evening, feeling worse than before. The walk home did nothing to clear her head, her mind feeling jumbled and messy.

As soon as she opened the front door of the house, she knew something was off. The air felt charged, the hair on the back of her neck prickled. She sniffed, the smell of smoke invading her nostrils and she picked up the big umbrella from the stand in the hallway.

Holding it up like a baseball bat, she crept through the house, eyes searching for any sign of an intruder. Everything was in place, as it had always been and she felt her heart thudding in her chest.

She turned into her dad's office, rounding the corner but hiding in the doorway, and heard a creak in the floorboards. Without another thought, she swung the umbrella with all her strength and it collided with something hard.

"Ouch!"

Mary stepped out of the shadows to see Dante rubbing the back of his arm as he glared at her. He was standing by her dad's desk, book in hand. Mary still held the umbrella up, challenging him with her eyes.

"What are you doing in my house?! How did you even get in?" Mary was not only shocked, but also maddened that

Dante followed her around everywhere. She couldn't escape him it seemed. She tried to ignore the quick thud of her heart in her chest and the way her skin tingled when he was around.

Looking Mary up and down with lazy eyes that burned into her skin, Dante grinned slowly and she remembered she was in sweats and a hoodie, feet stuffed into old sneakers. She looked a mess and she vaguely wondered why she cared what she looked like around Dante.

"Your dad reads some interesting stuff." He snapped shut the book between his hands and put it back on the desk with a thump.

"What are you doing here? Seriously, I've had an awful day and I don't want to deal with you too."

Mary slumped down in the armchair opposite the desk after realizing Dante didn't pose an instant threat, she was tired and fed up with the whole day.

"Well it's pretty obvious why I'm here, isn't it?"

"Why can't you just leave me alone?" Mary sighed quietly, rubbing her hands over her face, she closed her eyes a moment, her fingers gently massaging her temples.

Dante watched her thoughtfully. He was drawn to her and although he had a mission here on Earth, he wanted to touch her to alleviate her pain, if only to give it back to her in a way she'd enjoy. His thoughts confused him as much as Mary's did when she felt his gaze on her, making her body burn up.

He stepped over the uneven piles of books and crouched in front of her, feeling this sudden urge to catch a glimpse of those starlight eyes that made him feel things he couldn't understand.

Instantly her eyes snapped open, scrambling up and not realizing Dante was so close, Mary tripped over his knees and they went crashing onto the floor with a few piles of books with a thud.

Heart beating double time, Mary lay on top of Dante's chest, straddling him. His red and black eyes burned into her own and her skin flushed, delicious heat prickling all over it. Her palms lay flat against his chest, her hips on his.

Panicking, she instantly sat up and rolled off, not wanting to think about how much she liked feeling his toned torso under her hands, how warm his skin had felt on hers, how he smelt of cigarettes and smoke and how much she craved it.

Dante relished the way her body felt against his. He wanted to tease her, get a reaction out of her and make her squirm, but she rolled off before he could even try.

"The book." She remembered why she'd panicked and leaving Dante on the floor, she bolted for the kitchen, double-checked the backdoor was locked, and ran back into the office.

Dante looked too big for the small room, his body was oversized as he stood in his black jeans, black t-shirt, and black boots. His tattoos swirled up his arms and crawled under the sleeves of his tee and Mary swallowed, averting her gaze.

Damn, he is hot and insanely infuriating, she thought before sighing loudly.

"You're coming with me."

"And what makes you think that?" He raised an eyebrow, not moving from his spot.

"Because that's what you're here for, isn't it? Me."

Mary had him tapped. He didn't hesitate as she walked back into the hallway and he followed her, footsteps thudding on the hardwood floor.

"We need to go to the church, my dad mentioned a book."

Dante's interest sparked, could it be *the* book? He didn't want to let on about how much he knew, so he kept his mouth shut and nodded.

Violet E.C

The walk to the church was relatively short, but Mary walked faster than necessary just to keep Dante at a suitable distance. Who was she kidding though, he was much taller than her so his strides caught up to her in no time. And that only aggravated her more.

He lit up a cigarette behind her and she rolled her eyes.

Old habits die hard, she thought to herself as he blew out a puff of smoke. She hated the way she enjoyed watching him blow out the smoke.

What was he doing here and why was he constantly harassing her? She managed to escape him for less than twenty four hours and now he was back. Why did the world hate her so much?

Seeing her dad's car parked outside the church, she walked faster, instant worry sitting in the pit of her stomach. She knew he was okay, but they said he'd been attacked outside the church, by whom? Or what? And why?

There were fresh scorch marks on the grass by the gate and she bent down, frowning. Dante kneeled beside her, watching her reaction.

Running her fingers over the marks, she could feel some kind of energy, a charge that she'd felt before from that blue feather she'd found at Dante's house.

"Something was here."

Dante studied Mary's profile as she touched the scorched earth and he realized that she didn't know anything.

And that changed *everything*.

Straightening up, he scoured the churchyard, his eyes settling on a wooden box seemingly thrown onto the path.

"Is that what you're looking for?" He pointed and Mary stood up beside him, squinting in the setting sun.

She opened the gate and walked in, eyes on the box nestled in the gravel on the path. She bent down, brushing her fingers over the box and it felt electrical again, but familiar too. Like

Inferno

finding an old toy you used to love in your wardrobe. Nostalgic.

Unclasping the latch, she slipped off the cloth layer around it and revealed the book. The cover was intricate and the book almost sang to her quietly. She turned it over in her hands, confused. It had no name on it and no words, just an illustration on the front.

She motioned Dante over and he hesitated. He stood by the gate but scratched his neck, looking worried.

Mary almost laughed to herself that the church made Dante nervous. Hadn't he mocked her for being God-loving? Oh how the tables had turned, she was very tempted to mock him for being God-fearing.

Placing the book carefully back in the box, she checked the church was locked up and made her way back down the path.

Bringing the book to him, the gate clicked shut softly behind her. Grinning, Mary noticed the discomfort on Dante's face. He did *not* want to be there and it made her so happy to see him squirm.

"Who knew Dante Enfer was so scared of the church?" She teased and he narrowed his eyes at her.

"I'm not scared."

"Sure you're not." She rolled her eyes and made her way back to her dad's car. The keys were still in the ignition, windows rolled down a little.

She handed Dante the box as she turned to open the door but he yelled, dropping it like a hot potato. The box thudded to the ground, bouncing on the impact. She spun around, hands on her hips.

"What-"

"It burned me." He snapped.

He held his hands to his face in shock and sure enough, his fingers were blistered and charred, even smoking a little. Her

Violet E.C

jaw fell open in surprise. How could wood burn someone? She tentatively bent down to pick it up. No burning for her. *Weird.*

"Maybe you're like allergic to the wood or something?" She was grasping at straws here, absolutely baffled by Dante's burned fingers. Was it even physically possible? Nope and yet, there they were, plain as day.

Her eye caught a glint on the ground just behind Dante and she slipped the box in the car carefully before walking over to a big oak tree and bending down next to it.

Her dad's silver crucifix lay on the grass and Mary picked it up gently before clasping it around her neck. She stepped back and felt a crunch under her sneakers. Lifting her foot, Mary saw her dad's glasses, cracked and ruined under her foot. She picked them up gently, holding them close to her chest.

Dante's face was still uncomfortable and he stepped back when he saw the pendant on her neck like he was afraid.

"Oh stop being such a baby." Mary laughed at his dramatic reaction, but his face stayed serious.

"Can you just... put it away? It freaks me out."

Reluctantly Mary slipped the crucifix into the pocket in the side of the car door and slid into the driver's seat. Dante sat next to her, face blank and unusually silent as she reversed out of the area and drove home.

∽

Sitting in the kitchen with the box between them, Mary and Dante studied it. The box itself was ordinary, just wooden slats nailed together, no markings, signs, or words, and yet Dante's now iced, painfully blistered fingers said something different.

Inferno

"So, is it like… magic?" Mary could hardly believe the words falling out of her mouth, but somehow they made sense too. She'd had a feeling about magic and otherworldly-ness for a while now. She wondered if Dante would think she was nuts.

"Something like that."

She sat back in her seat, watching him. She'd expected him to laugh in her face and call her ridiculous. But confirming her crazy theories meant they weren't altogether crazy and that scared her.

"What aren't you telling me?" She was growing more suspicious, narrowing her eyes at Dante who sat back nonchalantly, crossing his arms over his head and Mary averted her eyes from his distracting, bulging biceps.

"Let's leave it at that for now."

"No, let's not. Everyone is hiding stuff from me, my dad, you, probably Ally too! I'm fed up with everyone lying to me! Tell me something!" She shoved her chair back, it screeched against the floor tiles as she stood up.

Chest heaving, hands braced on the table, Mary clenched her teeth, face blotchy from her outburst. Dante's eyebrows rose and he looked amused, much to Mary's dismay.

"Okay, so I know a few things-"

"Like what?"

"Didn't your dad ever tell you it's rude to interrupt? Patience, Mary Mack."

The temptation to rip Dante's head off was insanely strong and Mary held herself back, her skin illuminated again and she counted to ten in her head, attempting to calm down. She slid back into the chair once she felt she had enough composure not to do anything rash.

"There's more than one plane like your precious Bible says. There's Earth, but also Heaven and Hell. They all exist. And within that, other beings exist; angels, demons, and everything in between."

Mary sat wide-eyed for a moment, she opened her mouth to speak then stopped, snapping it shut and thinking hard.

"How do you know that?"

"Because I've been there."

"To Heaven?"

Dante looked at Mary dubiously and she mentally cursed herself, of course, he wouldn't have been to Heaven, he reeked of Hell.

"Why did you go there? You're not dead... Are you?"

Dante shook his head, laughing quietly. His dark hair had become messy, flopping over his forehead like he wore it in high school. Her stomach did a painful twist as she remembered his relentless bullying. This beautiful man was the Devil in disguise and she'd do well to remember that, not get caught up in the heat of the moment.

"Irrelevant for now and no, I'm not dead."

There was something Dante wasn't telling her, something that she perhaps didn't want to acknowledge yet so she stayed quiet.

He watched her across the table, pacing, figuring out how to process this information. *Wait until she hears what I am,* he thought to himself, smiling internally.

"So what's the deal with this book then?"

"Ah this book, it contains vital information; how to capture The Oracle, an age-old prophecy, the secrets of the angels."

How could a book contain such information and yet she'd been blissfully unaware of any other world besides her own? Well, that wasn't exactly true, Dante had made her aware of something all those years ago with the smoke that poured off his skin and his strange eyes.

And yet, Mary was different too, always had been. With her

Inferno

unusual eyes, her bright hair, and her glowing thing. She'd known for a while, whether she'd chosen to accept it back then was a different story.

"My dad said we need to take the book to Pastor Nolan. He lives in the town next door, like a forty-five-minute drive?"

Dante's eyes found the clock above Mary's head.

"It's late, we can get it to him in the morning, for now, let's get some rest?"

Nodding, Mary sighed and dragged her tired body upstairs, still processing the events of the day.

A throat cleared behind her and Dante stood at the foot of the stairs, looking up at her expectantly.

"The couch is that way."

Mary pointed in the direction of the living room, shrugging and Dante frowned. He watched her trudge up the stairs and went back to the kitchen, looking at the box on the table. He'd have to figure out a way to touch it, a way to open it so he could take the book, but for now? He'd play the game by Mary's rules.

Chapter Twelve:
An Angel and A Demon Battle It Out in a Back Yard

Present Day

A thud in the night threw Mary out of her deep slumber. A shadow crossed her bed and her heart thumped like a caged bird in her chest. She fumbled with the light switch beside her, not taking her eyes off the shadow, and flicked it on, illuminating her room.

The red demon with gnarled horns and a long tail grinned at her, its sharp, black teeth making its mouth look bigger and more sinister in the dim light. Mary was panicking; *this can't be real, this can't be real,* she chanted in her head, but she didn't dare close her eyes. The demon watched her menacingly, tail swishing back and forth as it stood at the foot of her bed.

Suddenly it jumped forward and a blood-curdling scream ripped from Mary's mouth, probably waking up half of Neverfield.

Footsteps thundered up the stairs and Dante rushed into

Inferno

the room. The demon faltered, obviously surprised to see Dante there. And much to Mary's shock, it bowed to him, speaking in a language she didn't understand. Dante shook his head briefly and the demon grinned wider, turning back to face Mary with a sinister spark in its eyes.

She barely had time to think about the weird exchange between the two, scrambling around for anything to fight off this demon. She flopped out of her bed, limbs flailing around as she fell onto the carpet and the demon's tail traced across her feet, feeling hot and slimy.

Instantly revolted, she shivered but hastily looked around for a weapon. Mary's eye caught her wooden cross on the floor, it must have fallen off the wall when the demon thudded into her room and she quickly grabbed it, pointing it upwards, she mouthed a quick prayer and squeezed her eyes shut as the demon jumped on her.

There was a squelch, a gurgle and suddenly the room felt too hot. Mary cracked open one eye to see the demon's face inches from her own. She screamed again, throwing it off and frantically crawling away from its blank stare and razor-sharp black teeth. After a few moments, she realized it was dead, its face unmoving. Her cross protruded from its chest, thick black substance oozing from the wound and dripping onto her carpet.

Her stomach heaved as she stared at the demon, not sure if it was really dead.

Dante watched from the door as Mary's face was a mask of horror. He could have helped her, but he didn't need anyone who could be watching, reporting back that he'd helped kill one of his own, it was better that he just watched.

She looked up as Dante and he knelt down next to her. She was shaking like a leaf, heart still pounding in her chest and he sighed, something involuntarily softening in his chest. She made him weak and he didn't like that.

"More will come Mary Mack, you better be prepared."

∼

"Again." Dante roared as Mary rolled over, heaved a breath, and pushed herself up from the grass. She was sweaty, muddy, and exhausted, but she'd insisted that they train today.

After the demon attack last night, Mary'd got little sleep. Anytime she'd closed her eyes, its red face and sharp teeth haunted her dreams so she'd given up sleeping and got up at 5 am to shower. She needed Dante's help to make sure she was never caught defenseless with a demon again. It had taken much persuasion to get Dante to help train her, at least in some form of demon self-defense.

She'd been to visit her dad while Dante had run some errands. He was recovering, but slowly. She omitted the demon attack last night or Dante's appearance, deciding he needn't worry any more than necessary and Mary assured him that she'd get the book to Pastor Nolan that very day. She said he'd check up on him again later and he'd smiled through his dry lips.

She and Dante had eaten breakfast in silence, staring at the box on the table, both thinking the same thing: if that demon knew the box was here then more would and they needed to be ready.

He'd very begrudgingly told her about the demons wanting to get their hands on the book, albeit not much information for her to use. She'd pieced together last night's attack and Dante's knowledge on demons and come to the conclusion that he was useful to have by her side. For now.

Standing up again, Mary swung her left fist at Dante but he blocked her punch, counteracting it, and caught her other arm, swinging her over and down onto the ground again. Her

Inferno

body hit it with impact and the breath left her chest as she took a moment, before heaving herself up from the dirt. She brushed a few stray strands of hair from her eyes and cracked her neck, ready to fight again.

She uppercut him, catching his chin but he was fast, pushing her back with a punch that would surely leave a bruise. She stamped on his foot before catching him in the soft place between his kneecap. Grunting at the impact, he pulled her close, his hot breath on her damp skin. Her heart pounded and his eyes burned black as their bodies were flush. Wearing nothing but a sports crop top and leggings, Mary could feel Dante's fingers gripping the bare skin of her waist. His touch scorched her flesh and she throbbed with need as his pink lips parted, his gaze setting her alight.

Their lips ghosted each other's, breath mingling, and Mary was caught up in a lust-filled haze. Blood roared in her ears and she ran her finger along Dante's stubble, outlining his jawline. Heart thudding in her chest, she almost wanted to give in, to taste that forbidden fruit. His mouth ached for hers, to feel her kiss. She ran her tongue across her lips and Dante almost groaned out loud.

He was caught off guard as she brought her left knee up, ramming it between his legs, and his face contorted in pain. He crumpled to his knees and groaned.

"Fuck, that was a cheap shot." He panted, hands cupping his crown jewels and Mary laughed, walking over to the bench to get her water as she rubbed the sweat out of her eyes.

"Yep, but it works every time." She grinned and chugged down a bottle of water.

"Unless demons don't have-"

"No, they do. It'll work." Dante snarled and Mary laughed again.

"Let me find you some ice." She headed inside to get an ice

pack, rummaging in the freezer.

"I hope frozen peas are okay." She yelled out through the window and Dante shot her a look. She giggled, happy with her "cheap shot" because damn, was that a long time coming.

She turned around and a scream caught in her throat as Turiel sat at the kitchen table, staring at the box. Mary blinked a few times, surprised to see him. She hadn't spoken to nor seen him since the night of the end of school party and he hadn't changed much. He was taller, broader, and just as beautiful as before with his white hair and silver eyes. So ethereal that her breath was taken away for a moment.

He looked up and smiled, Mary smiled softly back, her heart skipping a beat at his stunning face. He felt familiar like ten years hadn't passed and they'd not aged either.

"Turiel." She whispered and he stood up, walking over to her so softly that it looked like he was almost floating.

"Mary, I've come to warn you, something's coming."

What? She hadn't seen this dude in ten years and then he tells her 'something's coming- literally, nothing else? *Could he be any more vague if he tried?* She grumbled to herself.

"Seriously, my fucking balls hurt-" Dante muttered and froze when he saw Turiel standing in the kitchen next to Mary.

"Who the fuck are you?"

Turiel didn't react and simply looked back at Mary. She stumbled for a moment, forgetting that Dante was in the yard and that she was in the presence of two extremely different, but extremely attractive men.

"Uh, yeah. Turiel, this is Dante, we went to high school together. Dante, this is Turiel, we met a few years ago."

Turiel's face searched hers, not even turning to look at Dante and she felt weirdly analyzed. Her skin skin flushed under his gaze, she felt guilty, like a kid who had stolen candy.

Inferno

"Why's he here?" Dante looked at Mary and she swallowed, sensing the rising tension between the two.

"I could ask you the same, demon."

Mary gasped at Turiel's tone but gaped at Dante, his eyes flickered to her for a moment before hardening as he stared down Turiel. He had more than a few feet on the man next to her and she knew he used his muscle mass to intimidate. Dante was tall, ripped, and looked like he wanted to smash his fist into Turiel's pretty face.

Dante was a demon. She guessed it made sense, but it didn't hurt any less. The things she'd let him do to her, the things she was going to let him do, images of the demon she'd killed the night before flooded her mind and she accidentally visualized making out with it. She shook her head, thoroughly grossed out with her thoughts.

"Let's take this outback."

"Would love to." Dante bared his teeth like a primal warrior as Turiel gracefully walked out of the kitchen and into the backyard.

Mary followed behind, unsure of what to do. Should she intervene? Would Turiel be okay? Would Dante? Why was she so worried about a demon? She should be worried about Turiel, right?

"Checking in with your kind then, Angel? I thought you despised the Nephilim." Dante cracked his knuckles as Turiel stood a few feet away from him, watching the huge demon in front of him with sharp eyes.

Nephilim? Mary'd heard that word before, but where and when? Her mind was reeling with this new information.

Turiel's face remained impassive like nothing could affect him but he watched the demon's every move. He was big, yes, but also clumsy with his weight and fueled by his ego. Dante charged forward, roaring as he barreled into the angel.

Stepping to the left, Turiel missed the demon by a second and he skidded to a halt, turning around, eyes furious. He was physically stronger, but the angel was more agile and nimble.

It took a moment, but Turiel began to glow, like actually glow and Mary had to blink a few times to make sure she wasn't seeing things.

He glowed as she glowed.

Okay, she needed to sit all of them down and talk this out because she was completely confused. Not only was Dante a supernatural creature from Hell, but now Turiel was an angel from Heaven? Could this day get *any* weirder?

The angel raised his arm to block Dante's large fist which was directed at his face and the demon's skin singed as his hand wrapped around Turiel's forearm, sizzling like cold meat in a hot pan. When Dante pulled his hand away, it was red and blistered.

Mary started feeling angsty, she could sense the energy in the backyard, like it was a physical, pulsing being around her. She was jittery and when she looked down at her hands, they glowed like Turiel's. She didn't know what was going on, but she needed answers and she needed them now.

Stepping away from the angel to give him some space, Dante flicked his palm at Turiel and a stream of fire hit him straight in the chest. Mary gasped as he flipped backward, but he landed on his feet. He was undamaged physically apart from his white t-shirt which had a gaping, smoking hole in the center, revealing his milky skin and toned abs.

Mary had a hard time looking away as he glowed brighter, almost painfully so and she tried to shield her eyes with her hand. It was like staring straight at the sun. He snapped his fingers and Dante's skin blistered again even more. He yelled out in pain as he sank to his knees.

The smell of burnt skin and smoke began to fill the air and

Inferno

Mary gagged, suddenly aware the Turiel wasn't stopping. Dante's skin was unrecognizable; red, blistered, and sore, even on his gorgeous face. Mary noticed dark tendrils of smoke snaking across the yard from Dante's hands.

One black wisp grabbed the angel's ankle and flipped him again, Turiel's glow momentarily stopped and he jumped back onto his feet, but Dante's dark smoke was dimming his glow fast, it was sucking the light out of him, literally. Turiel was looking pale and grey-toned, his skin sallow as he stumbled forward, matching Dante's position on his knees. They mirrored each other at each end of the yard; light and dark.

Mary couldn't take it, neither of them was supposed to get hurt, she needed both right now and they were having a pissing contest in her backyard with magical powers. Enough was enough.

Letting go of all the pent-up energy inside her, Mary screamed. It knocked both of them off their knees like an explosion across the yard. Turiel fell back onto the grass and Dante's back hit a tree trunk. The trees trembled, leaves fell to the ground, the earth shook and Mary slumped down, suddenly exhausted.

After a moment, they stood up cautiously, both watching her slide down onto the step by the door. Her skin still glowed slightly, but her eyes were surrounded by dark circles and her skin, much like Turiel's, was washed in a grey tone.

He was first by her side, holding her hand gently and their skin glowed together. She already felt better as soon as he touched her, the color returning to her face quickly.

"Mary, look at me."

She glanced up and Turiel brushed her hair from her cheek gently, tucking it behind her ear. His fingers felt soft and cool, like getting into a hot bath after a long day. He smiled softly and she sighed into his touch.

"You used up your powers too quickly. You need to practice, you can't burn out like that again. It's dangerous for you."

Powers? Practice? Mary's brain was running at a hundred miles per hour, trying to make head or tail of this bizarre situation. She had powers? That's what the energy was inside of her and that's why she glowed. Her brain tried to make sense of it, but she was so tired, her eyes already starting to close, she had to blink hard to stay awake.

Dante slumped down next to her, his skin slowly healing of its own accord and returning to normal, the smell of smoke invaded Mary's nose, but the blisters and welts were healing, scabbing over. He eyed Turiel warily, differently from how he'd approached the angel at first. He underestimated his power; a mistake he wouldn't make again.

"Why are you here?" The angel asked, leaning on the wall beside Mary, still holding her hand and Dante watched at the glow between them. He'd never seen an angel give energy to another before. A flare of jealousy sparked in his chest, he wanted to be the one to hold Mary's hand. He squashed the unwanted emotion down.

"Same reason you are."

Turiel watched Dante and noticed his eyes flick to Mary for a second, softening as they did, he caught Dante's look and he knew it all too well.

"Shouldn't you be returning home?"

"Shouldn't you?" He countered.

Dante raised his eyebrows at Turiel and the angel sighed, breaking the connection between him and Mary. Her shoulders slumped but at least her skin was looking healthier.

"Unfortunately, the demon is right. I can't stay, Mary."

Her head throbbed, it felt like it had been filled with cotton wool and Mary looked up at Turiel, frowning. She was exhausted and like she could just fall asleep right on that step,

Inferno

but she had so many questions for him.

"Rest and we'll see each other again soon." Turiel kissed the top of her head before disappearing into thin air.

"You've got some weird friends, Mary Mack, I'll give you that."

A small laugh broke out of her chest and she sighed. What was her life like now? An angel and a demon had battled it out in her backyard. That sounded like a page from a storybook.

∼

"Mother Mary, I made dinner," Dante yelled up the stairs and she called back that she'd be down in five. She'd sat in the bath all afternoon, staring at the wall, contemplating everything, literally everything.

And when the bathwater got cold, she refilled it, her fingers wrinkling and her hair floating on the surface of the water like a mirage. Her skin had gone back to normal pretty soon after Turiel left, but her hair was silver again, somehow her burst of powers had removed all the cheap dye from her locks, not that it mattered anymore. She couldn't hide who she was anymore and pretend she was 'normal Mary'. She'd been hiding for too long.

Begrudgingly, Mary climbed out of the bath, dragging her lead-filled body to her bedroom to change. Her body ached like she'd just been hit by a truck, multiple times and she was so tired that her eyes barely stayed open.

She'd wanted to visit her dad again that afternoon, but Dante had told her to stay put because she looked like "crap and might scare everyone in the hospital", including her dad. He was just so lovely and polite.

Throwing on a hoodie and sweats, she slowly crawled down the stairs to the dinner table where Dante had set two plates of blackened mush.

She pressed her lips together to stop herself from laughing when she realized it was supposed to be spaghetti and meatballs, but it was burned to a crisp and pretty much unrecognizable.

"Don't say anything, it tastes better than it looks." He sat opposite her, looking too big for the chair, and dug his fork into the plate. He shoved a mouthful in before wincing and pretending to smile. It looked more like a grimace.

Mary couldn't hold it in anymore and the laughter burst from her, making her feel light and airy. She laughed until her belly ached, Dante grinned and joined in after a moment, spitting out the burned food and hastily gulping down a whole glass of water, which only resulted in Mary laughing even more.

She grabbed the plates and scraped them into the trash before dialing their local pizza place and ordering for both her and Dante.

He seemed to be staying at her house for now, which was some unspoken agreement that she surprisingly didn't mind, considering his house was nothing but ashes on top of the hill. Sure there were motels in town but Mary didn't want to be by herself, not when she knew there were more than just bad humans lurking around.

"What happened to your house?" She asked as they sat at the table sharing a large pizza. Dante had eaten most of it but Mary didn't complain, in a way, she found his company weirdly enjoyable. She decided to tuck that thought away, for now, she didn't want to start getting weak just because he'd shown her a soft side. He was still an asshole.

"It burned down."

She rolled her eyes at his answer, Dante had trouble answering a question properly, he seemed to always find a way

Inferno

around it if he didn't want to talk about it.

"I know that, but what actually happened?"

"I had fought with an assassin, I kicked his ass and he didn't win obviously." Dante grinned a rare, genuine smile and Mary felt herself smiling back before she could realize it. He was breathtakingly gorgeous when he wasn't trying to push everyone away or kill anyone.

He'd stopped styling his hair back, wearing it loose and shaggy around his face. It reminded her of teenage Dante, the cocky asshole. Nothing had changed and yet, everything had. She no longer hated him with every fiber in her body and she didn't know what to think of that. Somewhere along the road, he'd started breaking down the walls around her heart.

"Will you teach me?"

"Teach you what?"

"How to manage my powers." She felt stupid for even saying the words out loud. She'd have asked Turiel first, you know, him being an angel and all but he'd left in a hurry and she was stuck with Hellboy here.

Dante hesitated, he didn't want to admit to Mary that he had little to no experience with angel magic, that he knew exactly what she was and what she was meant to be.

She took his silence as reluctance and sat back in the chair, defeated by the day. This time last week, her biggest concern was selling a house and getting her commission and now she had been attacked by a demon, learned that there's more than one realm, and met an angel. Literally.

And then there was the question of her powers. Where had they come from? And they most definitely had something to do with her mom. She needed answers.

"Well, maybe the book can help us." She sat forward, the box's hinges creaked as she opened the lid.

Dante clamped his hand over hers. She opened her mouth to object but he put his palm over it. The smoke scent lingered on it and it felt warm over her mouth. He took his hand off hers and pressed his finger to his lips, signaling her to be quiet and she listened.

The floorboards creaked above them and her heart rate spiked as she heard someone in her room. She made a mental note to nail that window shut, not that it would make any difference to supernatural intruders.

Dante signaled for her to get up and Mary rose surprisingly quietly from the table. She saw him point to the stairs and he motioned for her to go upstairs.

Mary crept up the steps, heart beating loudly and quickly in her chest. She hadn't practiced with any of her powers, but she felt them swirling under her skin, ready to jump out, even though she was still exhausted. Her bedroom door was open ajar and a shadow flitted past it inside her room.

Mary took a deep breath and kicked the door wide open, feeling her powers boiling underneath the surface.

The demon spun around to look at her, its head was shaped like a snake, covered in dark green scales. Its forked tongue licked its lips as he eyed her greedily.

Mary put her hand up and her skin glowed. The demon shrieked in surprise and cowered as she stepped closer. Its scaled skin blistered like Dante's had done that afternoon and Mary knew she'd have to amp up her powers to kill it. A part of her felt guilty about killing something, but another knew that it was fight or flight and she was tired of running.

"Stop," Dante commanded from the doorway and Mary snapped her head to him, dropping her hand. The glow dimmed in her skin and the demon watched the scene unfold with curious yellow eyes.

"Leave, Jessamus."

"But Her Highness requested-" It hissed, looking at Dante with a confused expression on its face. They spoke in English this time and Mary blinked a few times, trying to understand

Inferno

that words, like *actual words* were coming out of this demon's razor-sharp and deadly mouth.

"I know what she requested, leave. I'll sort it out."

Mary watched in confusion as the demon stared at Dante, then begrudgingly put its hands together in a praying position and dissipated into a cloud of black smoke.

She quickly checked under the bed, making sure there weren't any other demons lurking around, ready to kill her.

"They're gone for now, Mary Mack, you can chill." Dante chuckled, amused by Mary's panic. She huffed and sat on the edge of her bed, staring at the dark blood-like stain on her carpet from the demon she stabbed the night before.

"You knew these demons." She stated and Dante came to sit next to her, the bed dipped as he sat close, heat from his skin radiating to her thighs and she found it hard to think about anything but him.

"Yeah, I know most of the higher-ranking demons." He said it matter of factly like it was normal to know all the demons that had tried to kill Mary. She guessed it was normal for him, but her? It would take some getting used to.

"Then why did you let me kill the first one?"

"Because it would've killed you."

Mary didn't understand but nodded anyway, not wanting to hear anymore tonight.

Dante got up and she assumed he'd leave so she could finally sleep, but he walked over to her desk. Her eyes followed his broad, muscular back, covered in a tight black t-shirt. Her skin tingled when she thought about his hands on her, how she'd love to feel the muscles flex and contort on his back as he groaned out her name.

"Where did you get this?" His voice was tight and it broke Mary out of her less than PG13 thoughts. His tone was sharp and Mary sat up, her skin glowing like an instant reaction to his guarded stance. Now she'd let her powers out and embraced them, they seemed to come naturally when she called.

He held up the big blue feather she'd found at his house, the one she'd kept all this time and she still didn't know why. Maybe because it was her only connection to Dante when the world had thought he was dead and even when he'd wanted her dead, she still found a way to remind herself of him. Yep, she was kind of messed up.

"Your house."

Dante spun around to look at her, his eyes narrowed and she resisted cowering, her heart beating in panic as her skin glowed brighter. He was back to the old Dante, the sensitive side she'd learned to like was nowhere to be seen.

They stared at each other for a moment before he broke his gaze, swallowing thickly. Thoughts of Ashja had rushed to the surface and made him angry, but it wasn't Mary's fault. He didn't want to undo all his hard work when he was just beginning to get her to trust him.

"It belonged to a friend." He said softly after a moment, twisting it in his fingers and Mary let out the breath she wasn't even aware she was holding. Her skin dimmed and she rubbed an arm, unsure of what to think of Dante's outburst.

"Keep it." She whispered and he looked up from the feather, eyes softer than before. She flopped back onto the bed, exhausted from today's adventures.

He nodded, and she assumed that was probably a "thank you" although it obviously pained him to say it.

He walked to the door, feather in hand, and turned back to look at Mary sprawled out on the bed, hair now as silver as the day he'd met her. She looked delectable and he wanted to do so many things to her, but Dante refrained. He'd bide his time, make sure she begged for him before he did what he'd been sent to Earth for.

Chapter Thirteen: The Forbidden Fruit

Present Day

Dante was conflicted. It wasn't often that he had a dilemma, after all, he was a demon and therefore morals were nowhere to be seen. But, something had changed in him recently. He wanted to help Mary, a part of him wanted her to be able to fight for herself. He wanted to help her learn her powers but he really had no idea how at least not without hurting himself and he didn't fancy being barbequed like today's encounter.

A real angel. He'd met an angel and he'd lived to tell the tale. He wondered why the angel spared his life, he knew it had the power to end him if it wanted to, but it stopped when Mary had told it so. He suspected Mary had the same effect on the angel as she did on him. Dante was getting soft and he wasn't sure if he liked it.

He was sent to the mortal realm for a reason and he wondered, not for the first time if he could go through with it.

He stared at the box on the table, contemplating what to do.

On one hand, he could send the book to his mother, but he needed to get it out of the box first and that would require Mary's help. Perhaps he could strike a bargain somehow. She was beginning to trust him but time was running out and he needed to get his hands on that book.

On the other, he considered keeping the book for himself. Maybe he could use it to overthrow the throne. *Now there's a thought.* It wasn't uncommon knowledge that no one liked Persephone's iron fist, but Dante wasn't sure if he wanted to rule Hell just yet. He had other plans first.

Frustrated, he walked out the front door, clicking it shut softly behind him. He was ready to burn off some excess energy and then maybe he'd be able to get some sleep. He grabbed a cigarette from the pack in his jacket pocket and flicked a flame on the tip of his finger. He lit it, inhaled a puff, and shook out his finger. He sighed contentedly as the nicotine worked its way around his system.

He began to walk in the direction of town, he could go to the park, maybe practice some spells, prepare for training Mary in the morning. He knew her magic would hurt him, but maybe he could become immune to it. If he was around it long enough, maybe it wouldn't hurt anymore.

"Dante?"

He looked up to see Ally leaning out of the top window of her house.

"Long time no see." She said, not smiling. He'd never had any beef with her, but after his unsuccessful drowning attempt, Ally wasn't exactly his biggest fan.

"Yeah well, I'm around."

"You disappeared for ten years, you're not 'around'."

He shrugged, not really caring what she thought. Ally was

just a human and irrelevant in the greater scheme of things.

"You stay away from Mary. She deserves better."

Looking up at Ally, Dante clenched his jaw. He didn't like to be told what to do, and especially not by a human.

"And you just stick to your drugs, then we'll both be hooked on something bad for us."

～

The smell of singed skin stung Mary's nostrils as she glowed brightly, holding Dante's hand. At first, she'd insisted on practicing on plants or the grass, but Dante told her that he needed to see the extent of her powers.

So, with great reluctance, Mary let her powers flow free. She'd accidentally let off too much quickly, resulting in a singed arm and half a blistered face for Dante. She'd managed to reel it back in before it damaged him further and he'd healed soon enough after she gave him an ice pack to ease the pain. He realized that he healed slower after her burn and the burn from the wood than anything else, and it only puzzled him more.

She stopped her flow of power, it was getting increasingly easier for Mary to control it at will. She barely had to think about it and the energy was there, centered in her palm and ready to go.

She let go of his hand and sat on the grass cross-legged. She stretched out her back. They'd been practicing all day and the light was dimming in the backyard. Dante crouched beside her, his skin already starting to seal itself together and smooth out the angry, red welts.

"Why don't I heal like you?"

Dante shrugged and Mary sighed. She wanted to know more about who she was and what her powers meant. Dante was no help in that department, seemingly to only know about demons. She guessed it made sense, considering he was from Hell.

Mary'd visited her dad again but he'd been asleep, she put his crucifix necklace in his hand, in an attempt to keep him safe from any more demon visitors. She'd had so many questions burning on her tongue to ask him, but she hadn't wanted to wake him up. So she'd stared at him while he slept, wondering what secrets he was keeping from her.

"Let's eat then we can practice more later, Mary Mack."

Reluctantly, Mary nodded, she wanted to learn more, but obviously, she hurt Dante with her powers so she needed to be careful. Once upon a time, she would have had no qualms in hurting the man who messed up her teenage life but somehow, in the last week, she'd grown fond of his company; he was her constant rock in this supernatural storm.

He'd been patient with her, helping her learn and not rushing her. Granted, he was snappy with her incessant questioning, but that was just him.

They sat down in the kitchen, Dante's plate piled high with chips, snacks, and sandwiches.

"So the 'daughter of God' could be any angel, right?" She asked whilst munching on her bagel, staring at the box thoughtfully. They'd decided to keep it on the kitchen table, considering no demons could touch it without being painfully burned.

Dante had told Mary a bit of what he knew about the prophecy, he'd kept the other details to himself, not wanting to give away all his cards at once.

"Yeah, it's not specific, that's what a prophecy is."

She paused, looking at Dante with a brow raised, before continuing to take another bite of her sandwich.

"And the 'Hellish offspring'. Is that a demon?" She said with

Inferno

her mouth full.

"No, it's a unicorn. Of course, it's a demon, Mother Mary."

"Can you stop calling me that? It's annoying."

Dante smirked, he knew Mary hated her nicknames more than anything which is exactly why he used them, he just loved getting under her skin. *Some things never change.*

"What's wrong Mary Mack? You upset?"

"Stop it." Mary gritted her teeth, she could feel the tingle under her skin, the power swirling beneath the surface, begging to be let out.

"Mary. Mack." Dante punctuated each word, watching Mary's face with glee as she shot up from her chair, glowing like a Christmas tree, and raised her fist to punch him in the face.

Although her powers were ready to be released, Mary opted to punch Dante instead of unleashing her power and potentially ruining the house in the process.

But he was quick and he grabbed her wrist, pulling her close so their chests were flush, and leaned down as he snatched her other arm, so she couldn't try and punch him again. Her skin burned him but he didn't care.

He held them above her head, wrists clasped in one big hand. Mary's heart thudded in her chest and her cheeks burned hot involuntarily at her vulnerable position. She felt every part of his body and her blood sang with the thought of what he might do to her.

"Remember what I said about violence, Mother Mary?" He ran a finger down Mary's flushed cheek, outlining her freckles. She glared at his dark eyes, gritting her teeth. His finger left a trail of fire on her skin, tingling as he traced her jawline and lips.

"Fuck you." She spat, angry that he'd riled her up and even more so that she loved the feeling of his body on hers. She

lightly bit his finger as he traced her lip and his eyes darkened.
"Gladly."

And with that Dante grabbed the back of her head and pulled her mouth to his. She barely had a second to register before she felt herself kissing back, eyes closing and giving in to the feeling of Dante. His lips were warm, soft, and demanding. Mary's heart beat wildly, her legs turned to jelly as Dante's tongue fought her own, he tasted of smoke and cigarettes. She felt the pulsing need between her thighs increasing, her underwear damp as his tongue fought hers for dominance.

His hand held the back of her head firmly, massaging her scalp gently with his nails and Mary groaned. Her skin glowed lightly, it was hot to touch, but not enough to burn Dante. It was different than before, her lust made her skin burn in a different way.

She ran her fingers through his dark hair, it was thick and soft under her fingertips, exactly how she thought it would feel. Her hands wandered down his torso, feeling his rock-hard body. She ran her fingers down to his jeans, cupping his hardness in her hand and he groaned into her mouth, pushing his hips into her.

One of Dante's hands held Mary's wrists, trapping her as he pushed her against the kitchen table with his hips. Her ass slid onto the cool surface and her thighs widened to accommodate his huge body standing in between them. His other hand pulled up her t-shirt and they broke their kiss as Mary peeled it off, throwing it somewhere in the kitchen.

They panted, chests heaving as they stared at each other. The smell of smoke filled Mary's lungs and she noticed Dante had a faint grey cloud around him. She glowed like a nightlight and Dante gazed at her. Her skin looked luminescent and her eyes were like liquid starlight.

Inferno

Unable to keep his hands off her, his deft fingers traced her stomach, the tips calloused and rough against her smooth, milky skin. Mary let out a shaky breath at his soft touch. She couldn't believe she was doing this with Dante of all people- she hated him. But she loved that she hated him, their passion burned together, it felt so right and she couldn't stop.

His fingers teased the waistband of her leggings and she pushed up the hem of his t-shirt, greedily stroking his rock-hard stomach. Feeling bold, Mary leaned forward and licked a stripe up his stomach to his chest. He grunted tightly, his heart pounding wildly in his chest. He was trying to hold back how much he loved the sight and feeling of Mary's tongue on his body. He wanted her pretty mouth *everywhere*.

"Tell me you want this."

She bit her cheek, determined not to give him what he wanted.

"Tell me you want my mouth, my fingers on you… in you," Dante spoke in a low voice and after a pause, Mary nodded.

"Use your words."

She stood for a moment, skin flush, just in her bra, staring at this masterpiece in front of her. And God, did she want him, every cell in her body screamed for him, the lust was all-consuming.

"I want this. I want you." She demanded, her voice firm, despite her racing heart.

Dante pulled off his t-shirt, revealing his tattoos, snaking up his arms and across his shoulders to his chest, covering most of his torso. Mary stared at him greedily, the dark ink turning her on even more. He groaned as Mary's hot tongue left a trail of fire. He needed her now.

Sliding her to the edge of the table, Dante pulled down her leggings and underwear in one swipe, leaving her just in her bra. He stood back for a second, admiring her toned physique. She worked out often, keeping in shape and it showed. He remembered their naked encounter in the work showers just a few days ago and he marveled once again at her beauty. But Mary didn't let him stare for long, she grabbed the waistband of his jeans and pulled him closer as he unclipped her bra, chucking it onto the floor.

Dante knelt down and any trace of doubt in Mary's mind flew away as he pushed her thighs further apart, teasing the soft skin with his fingers. She stretched her legs out and he hooked them over his shoulders before diving in and licking her folds. Mary nearly came at the sight of Dante on his knees in front of her and she scooted forward on the table, wanting more, but his hands held her still.

He teased her clit with his tongue, gently biting it and Mary's body jerked in pain and pleasure, as she felt his tongue lick it better. She moaned out, heart racing in her chest. Her hands struggled to find purchase on the tabletop and she gripped the edges, the hardwood digging into her palms. The tight coil in her belly was building up again, she felt herself dripping onto the table as Dante ate her out, making sure she felt every lick of his hot, torturous tongue.

She bucked her hips, trying to create a rhythm, but Dante held her down, only making Mary want him even more. Seeing her writhing for him made him so hard, he could barely stand it. But he couldn't give her what she wanted just yet, he needed to make her beg, to hear her beg for him.

Sitting back on his heels, Dante saw Mary pout. Her cheeks and chest were flushed with a rosy red tone and her skin was covered in a light sweat, she was so wound up and Dante loved to see it.

She looked down at him, eyes hard as he smiled smugly. His lips were glossy and wet and she nearly came at the sight of herself on him.

"Beg for it."

"No."

She panted, no matter how much she needed a release, she would never beg Dante. *Ever.*

Eyes dark, he stood up, towering over her, and slid his hand up her thigh. He teased her, tracing circles around her inner thighs before sliding one finger in and pumping slowly. Her breath hitched, she was so ready to come, her chest heaved, her nipples were tight and her white-knuckled hands gripped the table so hard she thought she'd break it.

"Beg for me." He whispered in her ear, licking her neck lightly with the tip of his tongue. She moaned, so tempted to give in.

Just as Mary was about to utter the words she thought she'd never say, headlights shone through the slats in the blinds in the hall. She hastily pushed Dante away, blindly grabbing her clothes. She ditched undies, just slipping on her t-shirt and her leggings again. Dante pulled his t-shirt over his head and he secretly pocketed her underwear, smirking to himself. His hair was slightly messy and she so desperately wanted to touch it, run her fingers through it again. She'd tasted the forbidden fruit and she wanted more.

The lock clicked and the front door swung open, Mary jumped away from Dante and ran forward to see her dad. He moved slowly, his legs were stiff after a few days in the hospital. Mary hugged him gently and he embraced her with one arm.

He stared at Dante. The boy had grown, he was huge with broad shoulders and thick muscles. Spells that looked like tattoos to the human eye, were sprawled across his arms. Alan had no doubt that Dante's powers were strong and he knew that he needed to keep his daughter away from this man if there was any hope of the prophecy not coming true.

Violet E.C

"You can't stay here."

Mary spun around, collecting her dad's belongings from the nurse who'd driven him home.

"Dad." She scolded.

"It's your kind who put me in the hospital in the first place."

She glanced back to Dante whose face was blank, watching Alan but not giving anything away.

"He has nowhere to stay." She said softly, still processing that demons had put her dad in the hospital.

"There are motels."

"Dad."

"Don't test me, Mary." Her dad rarely lost his patience, the last time he did was Dante's murder mission a decade ago. Mary knew she was walking on thin ice.

"It's late. We can sort this out in the morning."

"It's fine, I'll see you tomorrow, Mary." That was one of the first times Dante had used Mary's name without a jest attached and she looked at him, her heart feeling something she'd never felt before. They'd shared more than just lust not more than a few minutes ago and she wasn't sure if she was ready to acknowledge that yet.

"See you tomorrow." She said quietly.

Dante grabbed his duffel and jacket from the living room and stepped out of the front door, not looking back.

Mary watched his retreating form and closed the door behind him, her heart feeling heavier than usual.

She helped her dad up to his room and fetched him some tea before sitting on the end of his bed.

So much had happened over the past few days that she didn't know where to begin.

"Dad, Dante's helping me manage my powers, you can't stop us from seeing each other."

She felt like a teenager telling him about Dante, but she had to keep him close. She was too scared to lose the one person who'd kept her grounded through all of this.

"He's nothing but trouble."

Alan was surprised that the Prince of Hell was helping Mary, but he knew there was something in it for the demon, why else would he help his sworn enemy?

"There's so much you don't know Mary, so much I have to tell you."

He grasped Mary's hand, holding it tightly and she rubbed her thumb across the back of his hand reassuringly.

"I know Dad, we'll talk about it tomorrow. I'm just glad you're home safe. Also, I superglued your cross to the wall."

Her dad looked at her for a moment with a puzzled expression before laughing. She kissed his hand and left him to his own devices.

~

Dante chucked his duffel on Jesse's spare bed and walked back into the living room. He was mad; mad at Mary's dad for bursting in on a moment he'd fantasized about for years. Mad that Mary was strong-willed enough that she wouldn't beg for him. Mad that his heart was feeling something that he didn't want to think about. And he was mad that he had a raging hard-on that only Mary could fix, mad that the fucking book was still in her house.

"Hey man, want a drink?" Jesse, in human form, thanks to a complicated spell Dante's mother put on him, lay flat on the couch sipping beer from a bottle. He idly watched a baseball game on his TV.

"You're the all-American human dream, aren't you?" Dante snarled. He was antsy, filled with pent-up anger and he needed someone to be his punching bag, unfortunately for Jesse, he fit the bill.

"What?" He turned to face Dante and frowned. His face looked weird to Dante, too symmetrical, too even, too clean; no scars, blemishes, tattoos, nothing. It bothered him.

"Look at you, with your human face, human beer, human sports." Dante gestured to the scene in front of him and Jesse stood up.

"Oh, you're jealous, huh? You had to go back because you fucked up. Mommy called you home because she needed a real demon to stay undercover, not a spoiled Prince."

Dante's anger boiled over and he sent a fireball flying towards Jesse. Luckily the demon had quick reflexes and he dodged it, ducking to his left. The fireball left a hole in the wall next to his head, charring the paint and plaster.

Jesse raised his hand and his talons extended, slashing the couch as he jumped over it to reach Dante. The demon lunged forward but Dante reeled back, throwing a smaller fireball that caught the top of Jesse's head. His hair was singed, his skin blistered and he growled.

"Enough." A voice commanded from the fireplace and both demons turned to face Persephone whose face appeared in a cloud of black smoke.

"Dante, have you got the book yet?" She gave him a pointed look.

"It's still at the pastor's house, I need a human or one of the Holies to take it out of the box, it's blessed wood."

"And the girl?"

"It'll happen."

She said nothing but turned to Jesse.

"If he fails again, I'm relying on you to fetch that book and dispose of the girl. Don't make me come up there."

And with that, she dissolved into the smoke. If Dante was mad before, then this time he was livid. His own mother had publicly humiliated him in front of Jesse, who was already an egotistical dickhead demon.

Pushing past Jesse, Dante walked straight through his sliding doors, shattering the glass and ignoring Jesse's protests, he ran out through the backyard. He briefly glanced at the pool where he'd tried to drown Mary and wondered if he could do it again; kill her.

He feared that his heart was in deeper than he'd like to admit.

∼

Back in her own room, Mary sighed. She replayed her and Dante's kiss in her head, she didn't regret it though. Not one bit. She should have, but she didn't. Her body hummed with the need for release as she remembered what it felt like to have his mouth on her, to have his hot tongue trailing across her skin.

She flopped back onto the bed, staring at the ceiling in the dark. She tried to close her eyes, but all she could picture was Dante; his dark eyes, his full lips kissing her, his hands touching her body.

Realizing she was not getting anywhere with her thoughts, she decided to take a shower. Maybe giving herself release would help her settle for the night.

She opened her bedroom door and glanced at her dad's room. The light was out and she assumed he was asleep. She padded to the bathroom, flicking on the light and closing the door gently.

Switching on the shower, she stripped off her clothes and opened the bathroom cabinet. Mary grabbed her hairbrush and swung the door closed. She gasped as a dark smoke cloud hovered behind her in the mirror before Dante materialized out of it. He grinned at her through the mirror and she spun around, hands on her naked hips.

"Seriously? Do you not know what a lock is?" She whisper-hissed at him.

His eyes ran down her body slowly and approvingly, she resisted the urge to kiss his full lips as his tongue dipped out and licked his bottom lip.

"We have unfinished business, a small lock isn't going to stop me."

Mary's body tingled at the thought of their "business".

"My dad is next door."

"Better be quiet then."

She hardly had a moment to process before Dante yanked his t-shirt off, unbuttoned his jeans, and slipped them down his legs, along with his boxers.

He stood in front of her in all his glory, confident, cocky, and sexy as hell. Mary bit her lip as she ran her eyes down his tattooed, toned and gorgeous body. Her heated gaze made him even harder than he already was and Dante stepped forward, grabbing her head and kissing her again.

Mary's lips automatically responded and she slid her arms around his wide chest, feeling his strong back under her fingers. His hands slipped down the backs of her thighs and he yanked her up so that she was wrapping her legs around his hips. He stepped back into the shower, carrying Mary into the stream of hot water.

Their bodies were soaked instantly and Mary broke the kiss to run her hands through his wet hair. Dante groaned as her nails grazed his scalp. She was beginning to love that smoke scent, his black eyes searing into hers as she wriggled around his waist.

Dante wanted to make her beg again, but he knew he was on limited time so he pushed Mary against the tiled wall, their hearts pounding in their chests, their eyes locked and

Inferno

he slipped into her without resistance. She was tight and wet, and he groaned, biting his lip to stop himself from being too loud. Mary's mouth opened to let out a moan but Dante clamped his hand over it. What he didn't expect was for Mary's teeth to sink into his palm. Sweet pain and pleasure coursed through his body, making him jerk and he almost came, the painful bite of her teeth almost too good for him to hold on.

He began to thrust into her, deep, slow strokes to build up the pace. Mary's body was alight, she moaned against Dante's palm, her tension from their earlier teasing coming back in full force. She was wound up so tight and her hips met his thrusts as they both raced to their highs. Mary clenched around Dante, she was close and she sunk her nails into his back as she came, squeezing her eyes shut and screaming into Dante's palm. Her orgasm was intense, the sexual tension of the last few days poured out of her as she clenched. He came soon after, biting her shoulder as he released, his toned body shaking. They both stood in the steamy bathroom, covered in water, panting.

Dante slowly let Mary down, her legs were shaky and he caught her as she nearly slipped on the shower floor.

He switched off the water, watching Mary as she climbed out of the shower, her body was flushed, glowing again and there was a dark red mark on her shoulder, it would turn into a lovely bruise in a couple of days. He smirked, that was his fine work, right there.

She offered him a towel and they watched each other silently. Dante dried off quickly, slipping his clothes back on. Mary didn't know what to expect, were they going to hug? Kiss? Pat on the back for a good fuck?

Dante leaned forward and gently pressed a kiss to her forehead, weirdly loving for a guy who tried to kill her once upon a time.

"See you tomorrow."

Mary nodded and watched as he put his hands together and disappeared in a cloud of grey smoke. She gathered her clothes and padded back to her bedroom, keeping an eye on her dad's room for any movement. There was none.

And as Alan lay in bed, wondering how Mary had come to defend the very person that tried to kill her, he heard the floorboards creak as Mary tip-toed back to her bedroom. He knew he had to tell her the whole truth tomorrow. It was time.

A knock on her door woke Mary from her deep sleep. Her dad entered cautiously, carrying two steaming cups of coffee and a plate of toast.

"Morning." He said softly and she sleepily rubbed her eyes and pushed herself up. He put the coffee on her bedside along with the toast and sat at the end of her bed.

"Dad, you shouldn't have. You're supposed to be resting, remember?"

"Yeah well, I thought we both needed coffee, plus you were up later than me so I decided to make it while you slept. And also Dante is waiting downstairs for you."

Mary made a move to get up, but her dad stayed as he was.

"We need to talk first."

Finally, the talk Mary had been waiting for, but her heart ached to go and see Dante downstairs. She squashed those feelings as quickly as they came. She didn't want to even go there.

"Your mom, Eve, she was an angel, actually more than just any angel, she was an archangel so one of the first and very powerful. She was always hunted because of it."

Inferno

Mary stared at her dad, she'd never expected him to say anything like that. To be honest, she'd wondered where she'd got her powers from but she'd never assumed her mom had anything to do with it.

"You're half angel, half human- so Nephilim." There was that word. Mary thought back to when Turiel and Dante had fought, he'd mentioned that word. It made sense now.

"Your mom died trying to keep the book safe from people like Dante, Mary. He's bad news, you need to stay away from him."

"Dante's helping us, Dad. He said he'd help me with my powers, he's teaching me how to fight demons-"

"Have you ever wondered why? Demons don't do good things for free, they're selfish creatures who always have ulterior motives. You can't trust them."

"Well, I do!" Mary was exasperated. Her dad was treating her like she was five. She could make her own decisions on who she could and couldn't trust.

Alan studied his daughter, he worried about her blinded view of Dante.

"Mary, he tried to kill you."

"Yes, ten years ago, he's changed now. He's different."

Alan could tell he'd need to drop the proverbial bomb to get Mary to see the truth.

"He's the demon in the prophecy."

Jaw slack, Mary stared at her father. Dante couldn't be. Did he know?

"And the girl? That girl is you."

~

Pacing the kitchen, Mary contemplated everything her dad had said. He sat at the table, hands wrapped around yet another mug of coffee and Dante sat next to him. He watched Mary curiously, he'd heard their conversation upstairs. He knew what she was worried about. He knew everything. But of course, as Alan had said, he hadn't told Mary because he had an agenda.

"So, we're the people in the prophecy. But Dante-"
"Is the Prince of Hell." He grinned. Mary's face morphed into something of horror then to confusion.
"Prince as in…"
"My mother is the Queen of Hell, yes Prince."
"Why didn't you tell me?"
Dante shrugged nonchalantly.
"What difference would it have made?"
"A lot!"

Mary angrily began her pacing again, she was infuriated and betrayed. Dante knew everything and he'd kept everything from her, on purpose.

"Dad, what happened to mom?"

Alan sighed and Dante flicked his eyes to the man. He looked withered and he realized that he cared for this man in a strange way, he mattered to Mary and therefore he mattered to Dante. Man, when did he get so weak, caring about anyone but himself?

"Your mom, she died in order to stop Persephone from getting her hands on the book of Aeternum again. She died at the Devil Queen's hand."

Mary sucked in a breath, she tried to wrap her head around the fact that Dante's mom had killed her mom over a book. A book that contained information about a prophecy that alluded to the end of the world and her and Dante rebuilding it. It was honestly insane.

"Why are you here?" She turned to Dante who'd been watching her closely.

Inferno

"Why do you think?"

"I don't know Dante! I don't know anything anymore."

She slumped down on a chair opposite the others and ran her hand over her face.

"I want to speak to Turiel."

Having filled her dad in on the last few days, he was surprised to hear that an angel had been keeping an eye on Mary. He was told that all ties had been cut when Eve chose a human life over an angelic one.

"You can't just summon an angel, that's not how it works, baby."

Alan stiffened at Dante's pet names for Mary, he suspected they had grown close while he'd been in hospital, but he didn't want to think how close. He wanted to keep them as far apart as possible to stop the prophecy from ever coming to fruition. If they were together, Earth would be destroyed and reborn. If they stayed apart, then the war on Earth would never happen, or at least that's what he hoped.

"Then show me how it works."

This time it was Dante's turn to sigh, he knew they'd have to do power practice again and he was dreading getting barbequed again. He rose from his chair and offered Mary his hand.

"Let's go and practice then."

Alan watched out of the window as Mary and Dante sat next to each other. She glowed lightly and Dante flinched ever so often, Alan assumed Mary's powers hurt him and he was pleased about that. But he saw how they looked at each other, the little touches and smiles and he couldn't help but worry that Mary was under Dante's spell. The demon wasn't to be trusted, so Alan needed to be on high alert if he was to keep Mary safe whilst he was around.

"So if the prophecy comes true, we'll rebuild the world

together? Is that what the prophecy means?"

"Prophecies can be interpreted in different ways, but yes, that's what my mother seems to think."

"But what does that mean?"

Dante shrugged, he wasn't sure what any of it meant or even if he believed in half of it. His mother was so caught up in it, that it was all she could think about. Dante, on the other hand, wasn't so sure. Prophecies could be a load of bullshit spat out by fake Oracles who didn't know jack. How could Dante trust something that didn't even have a body anyway?

"Okay, let's try again. Focus your mind and visualize Turiel. Then send your energy to him, that's how you summon."

Mary concentrated hard, trying to think about her guardian angel, but all she could think about was Dante's hand resting on her leg. How it burned hot against her leggings, how much she wished he would touch her again like last night.

She shook her head and opened her eyes.

"It's no use. My mind's too busy."

"No, I think it worked."

She spun around to see Turiel sitting on the steps leading into the house, she smiled and jumped up to greet him.

"Mary." He grinned and wrapped his arms around her. Hugging him was like coming home. He smelled fresh and floral, his body temperature was just right.

"Let's take a walk, we have so much to talk about," Mary said and Turiel stuck out his elbow for her to take.

As Dante watched them walk out of the backyard, a possessive feeling overcame him. Mary was his. Not Turiel's, and he knew that the angel wanted to be more than just friends with Mary. He knew she felt the same way about him, last night had proved that but whether it was lust or something more, he wasn't sure yet.

∼

Inferno

"So this prophecy, can you give me any info?"

Mary and Turiel sat in the park on a bench, sipping iced teas. They watched the children in the playground running about, screaming, laughing, enjoying their little lives, oblivious to the war that may ensue from the realms above and below.

"The archangels bound me not to tell you, but you must trust your heart for what is about to come."

Sitting back, Mary sighed. She wished someone had a straightforward answer.

"And my mom, can you tell me about her?"

Turiel watched Mary, she looked tired still even though she'd been practicing her magic well. He'd been keeping an eye on her, making sure she was safe even if the Prince of Hell was at her door.

"Your mother, I didn't know her personally, but her death was mourned widely in the Heavens. She was cast out once she had chosen a mortal life, but she was never forgotten, many of us still watched over her and tried to keep you safe. You look very much like her, Mary." He tucked a lock of her white hair behind her ear and softly brushed her cheek.

Mary's heart fluttered calmly in her chest, Turiel's silver eyes burned into hers as he watched her expression. Mary smiled softly and Turiel cupped her cheek gently before dropping his hand.

"Was she allowed to choose a mortal life then?"

He sat back, gazing up at the clouds, almost as if he was staring back up at Heaven.

"No, strictly speaking, we're not allowed to engage in any type of relationship with a mortal. But Eve, when she met your father, she knew she'd never love like that again. As you know, she was an archangel and when you're one of the first angels, it means you've been around for a long time.

Eve had never loved another angel the way she loved your father. Their love was frowned upon, her visits to Earth monitored, but eventually, the other archangels turned a blind eye on their sister. I think they regret they ever did because Eve's death was such a loss."

Mary mulled all of it over in her mind. She truly wished her mother were here now, she'd know what to do, how to help Mary sort out her jumbled brain and her powers. The pang in her chest made her miss her mom more than ever.

It was late afternoon when Turiel bid Mary farewell as he went back up and she smiled, contentedly, knowing the Angels were keeping an eye on her even if it was from afar.

Chapter Fourteen: Mourning

Present Day

Mary stood outside the front door, fist raised to knock. She hesitated, contemplating whether to come back later. She'd come to apologize to Ally, with everything going on lately, she missed her best friend, her slice of normality and she hated how everything had gone down when they last saw each other. But Mary was also not amazing at apologies, she usually ran away from the problem rather than being honest and accepting that she'd done wrong.

And so, she stood at Ally's door, knowing she should apologize but trying to figure out how to. Sighing, she sucked it up, *any apology has got to be better than none* and she knocked on the white front door.

Ally's mom, Mrs. Chang, was on the other side and she burst into tears when she saw Mary. *That's not usually the reaction I get,* Mary was alarmed. If Mrs. Chang was crying, something had to be terribly wrong because that woman had a heart of stone.

"Mrs. C, what's wrong?"

"It's Allison."

Mary's heart turned ice cold and she felt her legs wobble beneath her. She gripped the door frame for balance, feeling a dark twist in the pit of her stomach.

"What do you mean?" She asked quietly, afraid of the answer.

"She... She passed away, l-last night-" Another sobbed escaped Mrs. Chang and Mary felt a hot tear trickle down her cheek. She was numb, hollow, empty like she was a shell, ready to blow away in the wind. She prayed that Ally was just messing around and that she'd pop out and say 'jokes on you'.

No. Ally can't be dead. She just can't. Her best friend, her rock. The world felt as if it had turned upside down and Mary looked around her, feeling like an alien, an intruder.

Nothing made sense.

Her whole world was wrong and the one person she could rely on to put a smile on her face was gone. She never even got to say goodbye, or apologize for all the shitty things she said, even make up for the lost time over the past years.

Fuck.

She hugged Ally's mom tightly as if to hold her together, to stop the pieces from breaking apart. Mrs. Chang ushered her into the living room where the rest of her family were. They sat and drank tea and sobbed some more. They held each other tightly and cried together until Mary's face felt puffy and sore.

She walked around the neighborhood after she left Ally's house. It was dark but she needed to clear her mind. She couldn't go home just yet and face her dad, feeling that the guilt weighing so heavily on her shoulders. She couldn't do it.

As she wandered aimlessly, her heart heavy with grief and

Inferno

her mind empty, she sensed a presence around her. The air shifted and she turned around slowly, trying to squint in the shadows between the street lights.

Staying still for a moment, she stared hard at the shadow but saw nothing. She continued walking through the park but kept her senses on alert.

A rustling in a bush to her left made her skin glow brightly and she stepped back, hand raised, ready to burn whatever demon had been sent for her.

A drunk man stumbled from the hedge, he stared at her for a second before strolling off, beer bottle in hand, slurring about angels.

Mary relaxed, aware that it was probably time for her to go home. All kinds of strange people roamed the park at night and although she had her powers, she was tired and didn't want to waste any extra energy. Her heart and mind were heavy with such fresh grief.

Just as she spun around to go back the way she came, a scaly hand grabbed her wrist from behind. Mary kicked her foot out, catching it at the knee and it howled as she spun around, body glowing and she put out her hands. The light shone brighter and the demon's skin sizzled. It was the demon, Jessamus, that Dante had sent away, she guessed he had come back to round two.

As she was about to give it some more power to end his life, another hand grabbed her ankle and she was caught off guard, her powers temporarily switching off as she fell to the ground.

Mary kicked the other demon in the face, with its black horns and purple warty skin. It had hairy legs, like a cow with cloven feet. She shuddered in terror at its completely white eyes, with no pupil or iris.

As she tried to scramble away, the other demon kicked her ribs, causing Mary to scream out as its solid hooves connected with her bone. She rolled up to protect herself and tried to focus on her powers but she only glowed dimly, she was running out of energy and fast. Her best bet was to conserve and scare these demons off until she could get out of there.

Lifting one hand up, she focused her energy on her hand, only her palm glowed as opposed to her whole body but both demons cowered away from the light. They didn't burn though and Mary tried to kick out again. She staggered up, her body aching from being a punching bag, one hand wrapped around her body protectively and she watched both demons who circled her hungrily.

Just as she was about to put both palms together, the purple-skinned demon was suddenly lifted off the ground and thrown into the night sky, followed by a fireball that burned it to a crisp midair. It barely had time to scream before it was nothing but ash, floating down from the dark sky.

Mary wasted no time in pushing all her power into her palms and she fried the scaly skinned demon in front of her. It burst into white flames before disappearing completely and leaving nothing but scorched grass where it had been.

Dante stood next to her, he pulled her shoulders close and she felt the tears well up into her eyes before she could stop them.

He put his hands together, still holding Mary and the air whooshed around them. They materialized in her kitchen and Alan jumped out of his skin whilst reading a book. He leaped from his chair and ran to check on Mary.

Before he could say anything, she turned to her side and vomited. She tried to apologize but her dad waved her off, going to find a bucket and mop.

"Yeah warping does that to you sometimes, you'll get used to it."

"Warping?" Mary wiped her chin before grabbing a bottle

Inferno

of water and swirling it around her mouth.

"What we just did, you know, where I disappear and reappear in places."

"Oh."

Mary slumped into the chair, exhausted from warping, fighting demons, and finding out her best friend was dead. *Oh, Ally,* she thought as a fresh wave of tears fell down her cheeks.

Alan quickly came to her side, holding her hand.

"Where have you been? We've been searching everywhere for you." His voice was sympathetic but also worried. Mary felt more guilt at the thought of her dad and Dante worried sick about her while she wandered around in the park at night like a crying idiot.

"It's Ally."

"What happened?" Dante asked, crouching down in front of Mary, one hand on her knee. He ignored the disapproving look from Alan who was tempted to slap the demon's hand away.

"She's- she's gone." Mary sobbed, hiccupping and sniffling. Her dad went to get her some tissues from the shelves and she cried even harder when her eyes caught the box of Pop-Tarts on the shelf in the kitchen.

"How?"

"Dante." Alan scolded, although he'd spent a fair few years on Earth, Dante's manners still left something to be desired.

"They think an overdose, they'll know for sure tomorrow. I never got to say sorry to her."

"It's okay, I'm sure she knows you're sorry."

"No, I said some awful things, Dad."

Alan shushed his daughter and Dante stood up, thinking about Ally. He had to admit that he also said a shitty thing to her the last time he saw her. But it wasn't his best friend, so he

Violet E.C

didn't feel particularly guilty about it.

Alan gave Mary a cup of tea and she dragged her heavy body up the stairs. She apologized profusely for leaving them so worried but they told her to stop. The guilt was eating her alive and she snapped her mouth shut after hugging them both goodnight. After showering and brushing her teeth, she flopped heavily onto her bed.

After a moment in the dark, Mary rolled over and stared at the clock on the wall, wishing she could go back in time and apologize to Ally. She wished she'd never said such mean things and most of all, she wished she could've swallowed her pride and said sorry before it was too late.

While she was zoned out, staring into the darkness, a black smoke cloud materialized at the end of her bed. Panic gripped her again and her exhausted body protested as she tensed up. Not ready to fight another demon tonight, Mary grabbed her wooden cross from her bedside and threw it at the cloud.

"Ouch," Dante whispered as he came into view, rubbing his forehead. The cross thumped onto the floor and Mary flopped back into the pillows, relieved that it wasn't another demon.

He was dressed in just sweats, no t-shirt and her stomach did a little somersault at the sight of him. His dark hair was tousled, hanging over his forehead. His ripped torso looked delectable and Mary wanted to do so many bad things to him.

"Scooch up."

Mary's eyebrows shot up as Dante squeezed in beside her, sliding his hands around her stomach and pulling her to him so that they were spooning.

"Are you- are we cuddling?"

Dante said nothing but rested his chin on her shoulder, watching her face.

"Who knew, big, bad Dante Enfer was a cuddler."

Mary giggled quietly and Dante buried his head in the

crook of her neck, inhaling her freshly showered smell and pressing a kiss to her skin.

"Shut up and go to sleep." He said, smacking her ass and she laughed even harder.

～

Rolling over in the sunlight, Mary felt a huge arm across her chest, a hand cupping her breast. She opened her eyes and saw the unnervingly unique red and black ones staring back, a lazy grin painted on his face.

His fingers gently massaged her breast, causing Mary to moan softly.

"Good morning." She croaked out, feeling her underwear getting soaked through.

"It will be soon."

His gravelly morning voice had her insides turning to jelly and Dante shifted on top of her fully, pulling her t-shirt up and over her head, exposing her body to him. He sucked her nipple teasingly, his tongue swirling around the sensitive bud before sliding further down the bed.

Grinning like a kid at Christmas, Dante licked a stripe up her inner thigh and dragged her lacy thong down her legs painstakingly slowly. Mary squirmed as his fingers grazed her thighs lightly, making her body throb with need.

Dipping his head down, Dante licked Mary's folds, enjoying the taste of her wetness first thing in the morning. He gently bit down on her clit and Mary's whole body jolted. She clamped her hand over her mouth to stop herself from crying out in pleasure.

"I heard your dad leave about thirty minutes ago, go ahead and scream. I want to hear how much you enjoy my mouth on you."

Mary moaned at his words and Dante licked her again before pushing his fingers into her, stretching her. She bucked her hips, begging for more as he pumped his fingers, but Dante was impatient and his morning hard-on was begging for attention.

He pulled out from Mary and put his fingers in his mouth, making sure he kept eye contact the whole time. Mary dripped onto the bedsheets at the sight of Dante sucking her wetness off his fingers.

He flipped them over, making sure Mary was straddling him, having shed his clothes before she woke up, he was naked and hard as hell.

Mary grabbed Dante's hard-on in her hands and he groaned, feeling her hands on him was sending him over the edge. He grabbed her hips and pulled her up to him. Kissing her lips hard, he pushed her backside down onto him.

She slid down slowly, feeling him stretch her at this new angle. Mary moaned and Dante bit her lip, tasting blood as he thrust into her. She slid up and down, savoring the feeling of him like this.

Hands pressed to his chest, feeling his rock hard body below her, she panted. They moaned together, their sounds filling the room and Dante came at the sight of Mary riding him, her body rolling onto him, her tight channel gripping him, her white hair like a curtain around her face. She clenched, pleasure rolling through her and came hard, riding it out as Dante still thrust into her.

She slipped off him and lay in the bed next to him. Her body felt relaxed, a thin layer of sweat made their skin sticky. He grabbed her thigh and pulled it over his hips, tracing patterns on her skin. Dante turned to look at her, noting her perfectly flushed cheeks and she bit her lip.

Mary'd been plagued by dreams of Ally burning in the

Inferno

flames of Hell all night. She'd slept restlessly, thinking of ways to free Ally and send her to Heaven where she belonged.

"Is there a way to free someone from Hell?" She whispered quietly and Dante watched her expression. Being smart, he knew what she was thinking already.

"Mary, I know you're sad about Ally, but she's where she needs to be. She was committed to a life of drugs and substance abuse."

She gazed at him, tracing his stubbly jaw with her fingertip.

"I know, but maybe there's a way. She doesn't deserve to burn in there forever."

He sighed deeply.

"You haven't met my mother."

The thought of meeting the Queen of Hell wasn't exactly filling Mary with warm, fuzzy butterflies, but she knew she needed to do something about Ally's soul.

"Well, perhaps it's about time."

∼

They waited for Mary's father to come back, sitting at the kitchen table, Mary tapping her fingers agitatedly on the hard surface. Dante was relaxed, watching her worry from the other side of the table.

He'd suggested taking the book in case there was a spell in there that angels could use to free Ally if his mother wasn't willing to negotiate. That had seemed reasonable and considering Dante knew more about the supernatural world than she did, she took his advice. So, Mary had taken it out of the box but carefully stashed it in her backpack. Along with lots of water because Hell was hot after all.

She was dressed in all black, with tight jeans, combat boots, and a long-sleeved top. She looked like she was about to rob a bank, not enter the depths of Hell.

"You realize it's hot down there, like fucking hot."

The way he said those words made Mary's insides turn to jelly. She tried to calm her excited body and focus on the task at hand.

"I know, I'm wearing this so I don't get burned," Mary said in a "duh" tone and Dante rolled his eyes. She'd be peeling her clothes off the first second they arrived and he wouldn't be complaining.

The front door lock clicked and Alan walked in with two bags of groceries in his arms. He did a double take before realizing that Mary was packed. Like she was leaving again. He opened his mouth to protest, but she cut him off, knowing what he was going to say.

"Before you ask, we're going to save Ally."

Her dad's mouth snapped shut with surprise. Of all the things he expected Mary to say, that was not at the top of his list.

"Save her?"

"Yeah, from Hell," Mary said it like it was the most normal thing in the world.

Alan put the grocery bags down on the table, rubbing his forehead. He hadn't had a break with his daughter recently, with her powers, the demon attacks, her best friend dying and now her mission into Hell, Alan reckoned he'd need a long vacation when all of this was over. Mary and Dante stood up from the chairs, grabbing their bags and hoisting them over their shoulders.

"Now, Mary, come on, be rational, you can't just go into Hell and ask to free Ally. The Devil is not to be reasoned with."

Dante raised an eyebrow but agreed. 'Reasonable' was not how he'd describe his mother.

Inferno

"No, but Dante is coming with me and he can help. Look, Dad, I know you'll argue for the rest of my life, but I need to do this. Ally doesn't deserve to burn in eternity forever."

He sighed, knowing when Mary had set her mind to something, she was very unwilling to change it. Alan wondered if he'd have an early heart attack sending his daughter to Hell willingly with the Prince himself.

"Fine, but take this." He unclasped his silver crucifix from his neck- the one she'd recused from the churchyard and stepped forward to put it around Mary's. She tucked it into her top.

"It was your mother's, it couldn't keep her safe, but hopefully it can for you."

He kissed her forehead and held her hands.

"I love you." He murmured and Mary hugged him tightly.

She stepped back and looped her arm through Dante's elbow.

"Keep her safe," Alan told him and Dante nodded before putting his hands together and disappearing in the black smoke, taking Alan's most precious belonging to the flaming depths of Hell.

∼

Mary coughed as she took a deep breath and inhaled a lung full of smoke. It smelled like sulfur, burning and rotting flesh. She barely refrained from retching from the sheer stench alone.

"Welcome to Hell."

A swarm of demons burst into the room, practically stumbling over each other as they gaped at Mary. She should have worn a hat or something, although it probably wouldn't have helped anyway, her hair made her stand out a mile away.

Sweat coated Mary's body quickly, dampening her clothes

and though she'd never say it out loud, Dante was right, she should have worn something lighter. She silently cursed him.

"Your Highness-"

"Take us to my mother."

They bowed and rushed out, a few glancing back at Mary ever so often. She stared back at the array of demons before her, all different shapes and sizes. Some looked friendlier than others, but she knew better than to trust any demon. Apart from Dante.

As they wound through the castle, Mary noticed the dank walls, dripping with a dark liquid she didn't want to think about and how they had no windows. Everything was dark and moldy, it smelled of smoke and death. She shivered despite the heat, her angelic blood revolting against even being here.

They entered The Great Hall and Mary gaped at the size of the room. Her attention was quickly drawn to Persephone, sitting on her black throne of bones and skulls. She watched Mary like a hawk, her beady eyes and dark hair making her every aspect of the Queen of Hell that Mary envisioned.

"Dante, I see you've brought a friend."

"Mother, this is Mary Lux."

She stared at the Nephilim girl, she looked exactly like the angels but didn't glow, *perhaps it's her human side that renders her powerless,* Persephone thought. *How tragic.*

"I don't care about formalities, why have you brought this Nephil to my halls?"

Mary gritted her teeth about being called a 'Nephil' but she stayed quiet, letting Dante do most of the negotiations, he knew his mother after all.

"A soul recently passed, Mary wants to save her, return her to Heaven where she belongs."

There was a pause, Persephone stared at the two before her

Inferno

then suddenly burst into wicked laughter.

"You want to save a soul? Have you told her nothing of Hell, my son?"

Dante's fist clenched next to Mary and she wanted to reassure him, but she also didn't want Persephone seeing her attachment to her son, she knew the woman was cunning and she didn't want to give the Devil any leverage.

"It's possible Mother, with your permission."

"And you think I care to even think about this soul? If she's in Hell then she deserves it."

"No, she doesn't!" Mary burst out and she immediately bit her tongue.

"Are you challenging me, Nephil?"

Mary glanced at Dante, his face was impassive as he watched his mother, but he inched slightly closer to Mary. Unfortunately for them, Persephone had keen eyes and a mean personality. Mary willed Dante to stay away, just enough so they could both survive this.

"You two seem rather cozy, have you sided with the Heavens then, son?" She sneered, standing up and walking down the steps of her throne.

Her heels clicked on the stone floor and Mary felt her energy glowing under her skin, she willed it to be quiet.

Persephone's eyebrow rose as she observed the Nephil with glowing skin, *now this is about to get interesting.*

"How is it that you can stand next to her as a demon and bear the pain?"

Dante hesitated before answering.

"I can't, it burns."

"Then why would you ever think that you'd be able to be with or even work alongside your sworn enemy?"

Dante grabbed Mary's hand in his, squeezing it even though it burned to touch her. He wouldn't let his mother take away another person he cared for.

Mary gulped as Persephone's eyes shone with victory, she suddenly raced forward, eyes on her son and she slashed him across the cheek with her talons. Black liquid oozed out of the four small, but deep gashes on Dante's cheek. Mary gasped, she tried to hold on but he fell backward, losing his grip on her and she turned to face Persephone who was smiling smugly.

"You're weak, pathetic, and not my son. You've fallen for her Nephil tricks instead of doing what you were supposed to."

Mary unleashed a bit of her power but it barely sizzled Persephone's dark skin. She looked at the girl with a bored expression and Mary began to give more power, angry at Persephone's attack on her son.

"Don't you touch him like that again." She yelled at the Devil and Dante caught her arm, his hand singeing as it made contact with her skin. He pulled away but Mary had already dimmed down her powers, her focus on him beside her. The gashes in his face had healed, leaving his skin stained with a dark liquid.

"It's okay, I'm okay." He whispered and held her hand gently.

Persephone, who'd watched the whole exchange, was intrigued by their relations. As she gazed at them, she had a sudden realization that hit her like a truck; they were the prophesied two.

They would bring around the rebirth and her demise.

Her son and this girl. How had she been so blind?

And obviously, Dante knew, yet he'd never told his own mother? He'd be paying for that soon enough.

Their connection, their sheer willpower to be together even though they were opposites in every way, Dante's obsession with Mary, was all because of the prophecy.

Inferno

Now she'd noticed it, she needed to act quickly to keep them apart, so that she could continue with her plan to take over Earth and not be thwarted by some star-crossed lovers. *Prophecies don't always come true*, she sneered.

She stepped down and closer to them, Dante had scrambled to his feet and he stood with Mary slightly behind him. The Devil thought hard before a sinister smile spread over her lips.

"You can have your worthless soul, Nephil, on one condition." She moved forward, her talon tracing under Mary's chin, so sharp that it nicked her skin slightly. She fought hard not to flinch and a bead of blood appeared on her chin, but Mary stayed stock still as the Devil stared at her, eyes black and red like Dante's, but unkind and hard.

"You leave my son here and sever all ties with him."

They both gasped, Dante, glaring at his mother with hatred in his eyes. He'd just found someone he cared about enough to want to save them, then his mother rips them from his grasp. It was like Bron all over again, and yet Mary mattered even more than Bron. Dante saw a future with Mary, he saw a life with her. He realized with a start that he'd never have been able to go through with killing her to stop the prophecy. He was in too deep.

"You see, now I know you two are the prophesied children, I can't have you ruining my plans of war with your silly, throw-away romance. So, I'm giving you a choice, Mary Lux; my son or your friend's soul which is burning forever in damnation for all the sins she committed, as we speak."

She squeezed Mary's cheeks between her hands, forcing her to look at Dante who stood stock still next to her.

Mary's heart thudded in her chest, she hated how Persephone had played this. But she should have known, the Devil was cunning; she was smart and she was pure evil. Mary turned to Dante and he looked as torn as she was.

His mind was a mess. On one hand, he was surprised it had taken his mother that long to piece together the truth, that he was the 'Hellish offspring'. She'd had her suspicions about Mary for some time, but her own son? She'd been too close to see the truth.

And on the other, he was annoyed with himself for even allowing Mary to come here on her rescue mission. It had been a mistake, bringing Mary and the book into the clutches of his mother. He'd still had ulterior motives but he realized that he didn't want to appease Persephone anymore. He didn't want to play her cruel games, he wanted to disappear with Mary. Start a new life together, just the two of them.

The Devil grinned, her black talons dangerously close to Mary's eyes.

"Make your choice, Mary Lux, and live with the consequences."

Chapter Fifteen: Ultimatum

Present Day

Mary stared at Persephone, eyes-hard and glanced at Dante who looked just as angry and confused as her. How could she choose? Her best friend's soul burning in eternal damnation or the man she'd fallen for?

She and Dante had a far from easy relationship in the past, but she really felt something for him now, something real, and Persephone saw that and she wanted to crush it in the palm of her hand.

The Devil stepped away from Mary, watching her like a hawk. She knew it wouldn't be an easy decision for the Nephil and she wanted to laugh at the pathetic look on her face.

She looked pleadingly at Dante but he wouldn't meet her eye, he knew she'd be torn and he didn't like the fact that he might be second best. He'd changed for her, and she was about to put Ally, the druggie ex-best friend before him?

Thinking hard, she stepped forward.

"How do you know of the prophecy?" She asked Persephone and the Devil rolled her eyes at the Nephil's pathetic attempt at bravery.

"Silly child, my Oracle tells me all."

Oracle? Like a fortune-teller? Mary tried to understand, but she was completely out of her depth. Oracles, prophecies, and having to choose between her lover and her best friend. She wished she'd never even come to Hell in the first place.

She watched the Devil with curious eyes. So if she had the Oracle, perhaps Mary could steal it, that way she'd have no extra information or power? She wasn't sure where it was located in the castle and judging from her journey through one wing of the huge palace, she guessed there were many other rooms and it'd take her forever.

Feeling distraught, she let out a frustrated breath.

"Time's ticking, Nephil. I won't be this generous again, so you better make your decision quickly."

How dare Persephone give her an ultimatum like that? Who was she to make Mary choose between two important people in her life?

In a burst of rage, Mary used her power and threw it at Persephone. The demons in the Hall flinched away from the bright light that burned off Mary. Dante cowered, shielding his eyes and feeling his skin melt like wax.

Surprisingly, the Queen's skin blistered, angry red bubbles appeared on her hands before healing slowly. Mary blinked, she was as surprised as the Devil was. Persephone frowned, her mask of arrogance slipping for a second. She had not expected the Nephil's powers to touch her, let alone damage her like that. She was stronger than Persephone had thought. A mistake she won't make again.

In an instant, her smile was back on and she laughed, looking at Dante, eyes amused.

Inferno

"I can see why you kept her around instead of killing her, she's fun."

Dante's jaw clenched but he said nothing. Mary's brow creased. *Kill her?*

Persephone's grin only got wider as she studied Mary's confused expression. *Oh, this is going to be good.*

"Oh, you didn't know-"

"Mother, stop."

"Dante was sent to kill you, but instead he fell for you. It'd be romantic if it wasn't so pathetic." She chuckled darkly, before stepping closer and drawing Mary's chin up with the tip of her razor-sharp talon.

"Don't try that again, my patience is wearing thin."

Mary didn't dare struggle, she'd seen what those talons could do and she liked her face the way it was. Her mind was reeling from the fact that Dante was sent to kill her. To finish her off and yet, here he was, helping her, going against his own mother. Or was this all just a trick? Mary couldn't make head or tail of it and betrayal stung deep in her heart.

Persephone used her thumb to stroke Mary's soft, milky cheek.

"I always wanted a daughter." She said quietly, surprising Mary. She stayed silent, watching every move from the Devil.

"But instead I got stuck with an insolent son who can't even finish a simple job." She raged and her eyes turned fully black, no whites to be seen as smoke poured off her skin.

"Mary, run!" Dante yelled and she didn't hesitate, bolting towards the doors even though she had no idea where she was going. The Devil was enraged, she flicked her hand at Dante and black smoke snaked out from her hands flinging him across the room. His body hit the wall with a thud so loud that Mary feared he was dead. He crumpled to the floor and he was knocked out cold.

Violet E.C

Mary screamed, her rage consuming her and she released the full extent of her powers this time and Persephone spun around, her robes swishing around her like the spirit of death. Mary's white light burned through her robes on her shoulder and sizzled on her flesh, creating large welts on her skin.

Persephone's dark purple and black robes swirled around her ankles as she hovered in the air and flew close to Mary's face. She smacked Mary's cheek and her powers dimmed, making Mary's skin normal again. She gasped, stumbling backward from the force of the slap. Her cheek burned red and she resisted touching her face and looking weak. The servant demons in the corner were cowering still, now more afraid of the Queen of Hell's wrath rather than Mary's angelic powers.

Mary tried to school her features, not giving away how afraid she was of this powerful demon in front of her.

"Choose." She commanded, her voice booming in the wide space and echoing off the walls. She flew over to her son, picking him up by the neck like a doll. He was still unconscious and his head lolled to the side. She extended her talons at Dante's neck, threatening Mary. If she chose Dante, they'd both die and if she chose Ally, she'd have to live with the fact that she'd betrayed her love.

Mary was desperate, she wanted to free Ally, but she wanted Dante to be safe, not caught in this place with his insane mother. She began to panic, thinking up ways to save them both but without Dante, she couldn't escape Hell. Dante told her she couldn't summon any angels down there either so Turiel was out of the question. She was lost, her mind spinning as she swallowed hard, looking at his crumpled body.

Having used a burst of her powers without much practice and in the place that sucked the energy out of her, Mary was weakened and she knew if she tried again, she'd only piss off Persephone more, she didn't have enough energy to even try

Inferno

to weaken the Devil. Her heart thundered in her chest, tears welling in her eyes in despair. God, she felt so weak.

"I-"

"Yes?" Persephone grinned sadistically, extending her sharp talons closer to her son's neck. She was hoping Mary would make the right choice. She didn't care if it cost her ten thousand useless souls to keep her son and the Nephil apart, to stop the prophecy from ever coming to fruition. Otherwise, she'd have to kill her son and that would be a pity, even if he was pathetic after all.

"I choose Ally," Mary whispered, barely able to speak the dreaded words. She didn't really have a choice in the end, but she knew Dante would never trust her again. A small tear slid down her cheek and she turned her head away from the man who she'd fallen in love with and betrayed.

Persephone grinned, her wicked smile making Mary's heart shatter even more. She won at this game and Mary was leaving her love behind. And boy, did the Devil have plans for her son, after she'd punished him for being so insolent and stupid, she'd turn him against Mary, tell him the story of how Mary chose a worthless soul over her supposed lover. They'd never reunite again and her plans of having Earth wouldn't be threatened again either.

She needed to get Mary out before Dante woke up.

"Zorax, take the Nephil to the Outer and find her the soul she's looking for."

The short red demon with four eyes took her arm roughly and they warped.

Mary tried not to vomit this time as they materialized in a place even hotter than the castle. Sweat dripped down her brow, mixing with her tears of betrayal. She took a deep breath, well as deep as she could in the depths of burning Hell. She needed to compartmentalize; get Ally out, cry later.

Looking around the space, she noticed it was a huge cavern with stalactites hanging down like sharp teeth, they dripped with a dark liquid and Mary gulped. She heard distant screams and wails, their echoes bouncing off the walls of the cave. She stood on what seemed to be a cliff edge and she didn't dare think about what was below. It was the epitome of Hell and Mary was itching to get out.

Zorax walked up to a tall, willowy figure, clad in dark robes that covered its entire being. The hooded creature sent a shiver down her spine. Mary wasn't sure if he was standing or floating.

He spoke in the same language Mary heard Dante speak to another demon in and she watched them interact from afar. After a moment, Zorax turned around to her.

"Name?"

She blinked for a moment, wondering why it needed her name.

He tapped his toe impatiently before gruffly saying:

"The name of the soul."

Mary was relieved, thankful he wasn't asking for her name so he could bind her here or something.

"Allison Chang."

Zorax turned back to the hoodied creature and they conferred again. She rubbed her arms, despite the heat and felt her knees shaking.

She reached for her backpack, grabbing a bottle of water. The bag felt too light and she realized the book was missing. She cursed under her breath. How was it that she'd lost the Book of Aeternum in the depths of Hell? She had one job to keep it safe and she'd fucking lost it. Mary wanted to cry in frustration. She felt her powers swirling under her skin but she willed them down, knowing it would be no use now.

She hoped that Persephone couldn't find it too, perhaps it

was better that it was lost or destroyed, then no one could use the power it held.

The willowy figure turned away from Zorax and let out a loud screech that pierced Mary's eardrums and felt like it reverberated inside her skull. She winced, tempted to cover her ears from the dreadful noise, but she didn't want to show any weakness. She didn't trust these demons one bit.

After a long painful moment, the demon stopped and Mary saw a pale shape floating up from the cliff edge. As it came closer, she recognized the face of her best friend. It was Ally at least her soul. She nearly cried with joy but held her tears back for now. Ally's soul floated to Mary's side, it looked at her with teary eyes.

"I'm so sorry." It blurted out and Mary shook her head.

"Let's get out of here first, then we can cry." The soul nodded and Mary turned to Zorax.

He looked at her blankly and she prompted him to take her up to Earth.

"The Queen didn't say nothing about taking you anywhere. You're on your own, Nephil scum."

Mary had had enough. She was sweaty, tired, and heartbroken. She glowed, using the last of her power, and stepped forward, towering over the demon. His eyes grew wide and he cowered as her crucifix slipped from her shirt and hung around her neck.

"You will take us back to Earth or I'll fry you like a little piece of bacon, try telling your Queen that."

The demon nodded, still cowering, and grabbed Mary's arm roughly. Mary snatched up Ally's hand and it felt cold. She shivered involuntarily, resisting the urge to let go and they warped.

They appeared in the park near Mary's house. She held back a wave of nausea, trying to focus on her breathing when suddenly a foot kicked her in the back. She stumbled forward onto her stomach and Ally's soul screamed.

"Watch out, Maz!"

Mary spun around to see Zorax throwing a punch. She dodged his fist quickly and thrust her foot between his legs. He doubled over and she grinned, but only for a second as the memory of her and Dante's practice fighting and his reaction to her move invaded her mind. She sighed deeply. He would never forgive her even though she hadn't had a choice in the end.

"That's for calling me 'scum', you piece of shit." Mary amped up her power, pressing her hand to his slimy skin until the demon burst into flames and left nothing behind but scorched earth. Ally cheered behind her.

"Damn, girl, you're a badass." She laughed and Mary smiled back sadly.

"I'm so sorry Ally, for everything. I'm a shit friend, I ran away from everything here, but I never stopped missing you. And you were right, right about the prophecy, right about my selfishness, right about everything." She cried and a tear slipped down Ally's cheek.

"It's okay Mary, I'm okay. I made some bad decisions but I gotta live with them. Just tell my mom that I'm sorry, she deserved a better daughter."

Mary nodded and held Ally's cold hand again.

"How did you get me out of there anyway?"

She sighed, not wanting to admit that she had fallen for a demon, but not just any demon, the Prince of Hell.

"I- I had to leave Dante behind."

"Good riddance then!" Ally cheered, but Mary shook her head.

"I think I loved him, Al."

There was a pause in which Ally saw the sorrow on Mary's

Inferno

face. She felt bad for her best friend, everything she loved, she lost. Every time Mary had someone to love, they got taken away from her; her mom, Ally, and now Dante.

"Perhaps it's for the better, he wasn't a good person." She whispered, unconvinced that Dante was suddenly a good guy.

"No, but he was becoming one."

They sat for a while, catching up on each other's lives, something they should have done years ago and as the sky painted pink, Mary knew it was time to let her best friend go.

She summoned Turiel with ease this time and he appeared behind her.

"Mary." He greeted and she hugged him. He smiled softly and rubbed some dirt from her cheek with his thumb.

"You reek of sulfur and death." She laughed as Turiel wrinkled his nose in disgust. "So you managed to do it. Save a soul and get out of Hell in one piece. I have to say I'm impressed." Mary grinned even though her heart ached and she pulled Ally's arm so her best friend stood next to her.

"You remember Ally? She was at the party that night."

"We briefly met." He looked at Ally and she ran her eyes down him.

"So you're an angel? Damn, my day just keeps getting weirder."

"Take good care of her, Turiel."

"Of course."

She smiled sadly at him, thinking about all she'd lost as she stared into his silver eyes. She gave Ally another hug, embraced the chill from her soul, and kissed her forehead.

"I love you, Al." She whispered as her best friend burst into tears.

Turiel took Ally's hand in his milky one and they disappeared together.

Mary watched the space where they had been for a moment,

before turning around to head home with an equally light and heavy heart.

Epilogue

Dante awoke in his room, on his black stone bed. His head felt fuzzy and he looked around, expecting Mary to be there.

Instead, Persephone sat on a chair on the other side of the room, watching him sharply with her hawk-like eyes.

"Where's Mary?" Dante asked hoarsely.

"She left you. I gave her a choice, and she chose her friend's soul." His mother shrugged like she couldn't care less, but Dante felt a sharp pain in his chest, it was like someone had hit him with a sledgehammer where his heart was. It hurt like nothing he'd ever felt before. The pain almost knocked the breath out of him. *Is this heartbreak?* He wondered.

He couldn't believe Mary would choose her friend over him. Did their time together mean nothing to her? He'd changed because of her. He was willing to stay on Earth with her.

His heartbreak bubbled into anger in his chest, he threw the covers off and unleashed a fireball at the wall. It left a scorched mark but did no damage and he didn't feel one bit better.

His anger still felt fresh, boiling over like a pot of hot water and he roared, smoke pouring off his skin as he let out a stream of fire which set his bedsheets and all the furnishings alight, cocooning them in an inferno.

His mother watched him for a moment, impressed by his power before clicking her fingers and the burning room returned to normal as if Dante hadn't just had a flaming outburst.

She'd betrayed him and he'd get her back for it. He'd do more than drown her in a pool, he'd make sure Mary Lux burned in the fiery depths of Hell for eternity. He'd been tricked by a human, a weak, pathetic, fucking human. Just like his heart, he'd been a fool, and he swore he'd never fall again.

"Although I love seeing you get angry at the Nephil, save it. Because now we have this."

Persephone brought something out from behind her back and Dante's mouth fell open in shock. Then a sinister grin spread over it as a plan formed in his head.

In her hands, lay the Book of Aeternum.

Now they had all they needed for their war on Earth.

Inferno

Book Two of the Hell on Earth Series is coming soon...

Stay tuned!

If you loved Inferno, please don't forget to rate and/ or review it on Amazon and Goodreads.

You can find Violet E.C on Instagram, Facebook and Twitter.

You can also contact her at violet.e.c.author@gmail.com

Acknowledgements

Wow, thank you if you finished Inferno! It's been hard work but I absolutely adored writing Dante and Mary's stories. Isn't their romance just the spiciest?!

This is my first ever series, so bear with me as I figure out logistics and whatnot. It's mildly terrifying to realize that I'm carrying a somewhat complicated plot over several hundred pages!

So here come the thank yous:

I want to say a massive thank you to my friends; April and Saskia. You guys are like my personal cheerleaders, always being the first ones to buy my books and I cannot thank you enough for your support! And to Laura, Holly, Nylah and anyone else who buys any of my books and takes the time to read it.

To my wonderful brother and typesetter Hal, again, thank you for putting the time and work in, it doesn't go unappreciated.

And to all my readers, wherever you are in the world- thank you, thank you, thank you. You help my writing reach different eyes all over the globe and I'm forever grateful.

If you liked Inferno, then you can let me know by getting in touch with me on my social medias below:

- **Instagram:** @violet.e.c.author
- **Twitter:** @Author_VioletEC
- **Facebook:** @violet.e.c.author

Or drop me an email at violet.e.c.author@gmail.com
Much love x

Inferno

Printed in Great Britain
by Amazon